About Amy Andrews

Amy Andrews has always loved writing, and still can't quite believe that she gets to do it for a living. Creating wonderful heroines and gorgeous heroes and telling their stories is an amazing way to pass the day. Sometimes they don't always act as she'd like them to—but then neither do her kids, so she's kind of used to it. Amy lives in the very beautiful Samford Valley, with her husband and aforementioned children, along with six brown chooks and two black dogs.

She loves to hear from her readers. Drop her a line at **www.amyandrews.com.au**

To

Praise for Amy Andrews

'With a wonderful heroine, a strong and sexy hero,
and packed with drama, charm and realism,
A Mother for Matilda is just the tonic to
cheer up die-hard romantics the world over!'
—www.cataromance.com on
Mills & Boon® Medical™ Romance *A Mother for Matilda*

'Whether Amy Andrews is an auto-buy for you, or a
new-to-you author, this book is definitely worth reading.'
—Pink Heart Society Book Reviews on
Mills & Boon® Medical™ Romance *A Mother for Matilda*

'A spectacular set of stories by Ms Andrews,
the *Italian Surgeon to Dad!* duet features tales of Italian
men who know how to leave a lasting impression in the
imaginations of readers who love the romance genre.'
—www.cataromance.com

Amy also won a RB*Y (Romance Book of the Year)
Award in 2010 for *A Doctor, A Nurse, A Christmas Baby!*

Innocent
'til Proven Otherwise

Amy Andrews

MILLS
BOON

First published in Great Britain 2012
by Mills & Boon, an imprint of Harlequin (UK) Limited.
Harlequin (UK) Limited, Eton House, 18-24 Paradise Road,
Richmond, Surrey TW9 1SR

© Amy Andrews 2012

ISBN: 978 0 263 89292 5

Harlequin (UK) policy is to use papers that are natural, renewable
and recyclable products and made from wood grown in sustainable
forests. The logging and manufacturing process conform to the
legal environmental regulations of the country of origin.

Printed and bound in Spain
by Blackprint CPI, Barcelona

This is Amy Andrews's
first book for RIVA!

If you'd like to see more of this author's
fantastic books, visit our website below and
check out her Mills & Boon® Medical™ Romances.

We're looking forward to
more of Amy Andrews's RIVAs—coming soon!

Visit www.millsandboon.co.uk

For Kelly Hunter and Anna Cleary,
two fabulous writers
who encouraged me to stretch my wings.

CHAPTER ONE

'Two shots of tequila and keep them coming.'

Aleisha Gregory groaned at Kat's choice of Friday-night poison as she reluctantly plonked herself on the bar seat next to the leggy blonde. Saturday night was usually tequila night and she knew from experience that the Mexican liquor had a nasty habit of making her friend's clothes fall off, usually with wildly inappropriate men.

Which was fine. Kat was a grown woman after all. Until the panicked phone call she always received at the crack of dawn the next day asking to be picked up from a strange address and the ensuing couple of days of vocal self-loathing.

'Think I'd rather have something with an umbrella.'

After years of drinking sessions with Kat, Aleisha had learned that cocktails went down slower. Besides, it was still Happy Hour and eight-dollar cocktails could not be sneezed at.

Kat glanced at her friend and tisked. 'Ali, Ali, Ali. You city girls, no stamina.' She turned back to the boy/man behind the bar. 'Make it two daiquiris instead. And if you could make them all pretty and pink you will hold a special place in my heart for ever.'

Ali watched as Kat batted her eyes at the bartender. His pronounced Adam's apple bobbed convulsively once, twice, before he practically fell over himself to fill Kat's orders. Ali wouldn't mind betting he could make a daiquiri with polka dots if Kat had requested it.

She rolled her eyes at her friend. 'He's a child, Katarina.'

Kat ignored her. 'Right,' she said, looking around the dimly lit, half-full bar, her keen eyesight scanning the offerings, probing into corners, assessing tonight's selection of possibles. 'Let's get you hooked up.'

Ali shook her head. 'Kitty Kat, since when have I ever hooked up?'

'Precisely!' Kat poked Ali in the shoulder. 'Maybe if you'd hooked up a little more often you might not have ended up with Terrible Tom.'

Ali winced. Kat's insights could be a little brutal from time to time. 'Well, I didn't end up with him, did I?'

'That's only because Two-Timing Tom is a jerk. Trust me, you had a lucky escape.'

Ali blew a persistent curl out of her eye. Funny, she didn't feel lucky. Tonight she was surprised to realise she still felt a little raw. Even a year down the track.

Admittedly, it has been a particularly heinous year.

The bartender placed their cocktails before them with a flourish and Ali watched him blush as Kat bestowed him with her you're-such-a-big-clever-man smile and then totally ignored him.

'What happened to your hand?' Ali asked the besotted bartender.

He looked down at the small red laceration gracing the back of his hand. 'I was trying to break up a dog fight this arvo.' He smiled at Kat. 'One of them took exception.'

Ali rolled her eyes at the lame attempt to impress. 'Did you get a tetanus shot?'

The bartender dragged his gaze to Ali. 'Er… no. Should I?'

Ali gave a brisk nod. 'Absolutely.'

He glanced at Kat, who shrugged. 'Okay, I will… thanks,' he said, before withdrawing to take another order.

Kat shook her head at her friend. 'You're hopeless.'

Ali sighed. 'Sorry, can't help it.'

Kat grinned, then lifted her glass and clinked it against Ali's. 'Here's to getting lucky.'

Ali clinked automatically but knew in her heart she'd settle for just getting through. Getting through this night without completely breaking down and ending up curled in a foetal position on her bed. Mostly she'd been able to put the hurt aside and get on with things. But knowing what was going on over on the other side of town brought it all back into sharp focus.

She looked into the creamy pink swirl of alcohol and figured that a few of these might just do the trick. She matched her friend's giant-sized swig with one of her own and felt the almost immediate slug as the alcohol hit her square between the eyes.

Ali placed the glass back on the bar. 'I can do this,' she said.

Kat nodded. 'Of course you can.' And she took another swig. Then she nudged Ali's shoulder. 'Guy over the other side of the bar, he's checking you out.'

Ali thought it highly unlikely anyone would be checking her out when she was sitting next to God's-gift-to-mankind. Seriously, why would a guy settle for Ms Average when he could take a shot at Ms Holy-Cow? But, used to humouring her friend, she followed Kat's line of vision anyway.

Okay-looking man. Nice suit. Nice eyes. Nice smile.

Nice. Nice. Nice.

Tom had been nice. In the beginning.

Ali sucked in a breath. Tom's betrayal with a sultry twenty-year-old redhead had shaken her perennial self-confidence and left her feeling old—at the advanced age of almost thirty—and ugly.

Before that particularly awful experience she'd known, the way a woman did, that she was attractive. Sure, not in Kat's league, but she hadn't been blind to the fact that men checked her out. She had good hair, nice skin, a size-twelve figure and a set of D cups.

But this last year, for the first time ever—thanks to Tom—she'd felt downright unattractive. His infidelity had hit her right in the libido.

The guy pushed off the bar and headed towards them. 'Oh, no,' Ali groaned, having another swig of cocktail. 'He's coming over.'

Kat laughed. 'Okay now,' she said hurriedly, reinforcing the ground rules. 'Tonight is about hooking up. About moving on. It's not about falling in love or happily-ever-afters. It's about you getting back up on the horse. About getting out there again.'

Ali sighed. 'I hated being out there.' And she had. She'd never been more content than when she'd been part of a couple. 'I loved being off the horse.'

'And how'd that work out for you?'

Kat saw her friend's face fall and was instantly contrite. She squeezed Ali's hand and dropped her voice lower.

'I'm sorry, babe, but you have to get past this. Terrible Tom is—' Kat checked her watch '—right at this moment, saying I do to the woman slash child he cheated with while he was engaged to you and you were pregnant with his baby. The very same Tom who broke up with you the day you miscarried, when you were lying in a hospital bed bleeding and sobbing, telling you he never wanted *it* anyway.'

Ali played with the frosty stem of her glass, barricading her heart from the emotional tumult threatening to consume it. She had to admit, as the guy moved closer, Kat made a very good argument.

'So I'd say you're well past due for a little moving-on sex. It's time, Ali. Tom cut you off at the knees. But it's been a year—stop letting him win.'

Stop letting him win.

Kat's advice, brutal as ever, ricocheted around her head. Did she really want to spend the night bumping bits with a stranger? No. But she really didn't want to spend the night thinking about Tom doing it with his brand-new wife either.

'Okay,' she sighed. 'Okay.'

Kat grinned and nudged her with her shoulder. 'Just try, Ali, okay? That's all I ask. And do not, I repeat, do not, diagnose some obscure medical problem the second he sits down.'

'Okay, okay. I'll try. I promise.'

Just try. Just try. It chanted in Ali's brain as Mr Nice plonked down on the bar stool beside her.

'Hello, ladies, how are we doing tonight?'

Kat squeezed Ali's hand and plastered a bright smile on her face. 'Fabulous,' she beamed. 'Even better now you're here.'

'And what are two gorgeous women such as yourselves doing sitting all alone at a bar?'

Ali shuddered at the easy patter. The guy was obviously well versed in pick-up lines. She braced herself for the inevitable where-have-you-been-all-my-life and studiously ignored his deviated septum and associated nasally inflection.

Just try.

And she did. For five minutes it was all going well. He'd even bought them another daiquiri each. And then he asked the fateful question.

'So, Ali, what do you do?'

Ali spoke before even thinking the answer through. 'I'm a brain surgeon.' She felt Kat tense beside her as Mr Nice threw back his head and laughed. 'No, really, I *am* a brain surgeon.'

Or at least she had been until recently.

'You know, a neurosurgeon?' she clarified for the grinning man, irritated by his obvious disbelief.

Mr Nice's smile wavered and then fell and she sensed rather than saw Kat's shoulders droop.

'Oh, right, really?' he said, checking his watch and downing his drink in one swallow. 'Well, um…nice meeting you ladies but I gotta…uh, rush.'

Ali watched Mr Nice retreat as if she'd just confessed to having Ebola. Kat gave her an exasperated look. 'What?' She spread her hands. 'I never mentioned his obvious sinus problems, not once.'

Kat raised an eyebrow. 'Neurosurgeon?'

'I *am* a neurosurgeon. Why does no one believe me when I say that?'

Kat sighed. 'Because it's a cliché, babe.'

'Being a neurosurgeon is a cliché?'

Good to know that a decade of study and killer shifts had been reduced to a cliché. Well, wasn't that par for the course for the way her life had been running lately?

Not that it mattered because she was never going back. Ever.

'No, babe. The line's a cliché.' Kat looked at her friend and sighed again. 'Ali, you gotta know that intimidates men.'

Ali rolled her eyes. 'I don't have time in my life for cavemen, Kitty Kat.'

'Tonight you do, babe. Tonight you do.'

Ali shook her head. 'Oh, I don't know Kat… I've never been very good at this.'

Kat grinned. 'Well, lucky for you, I am. Now trust me on this, let's just stick with your current occupation, okay? Remember, the coffee shop?'

Ali hesitated pulling her bottom lip between her teeth. *How could she forget?*

'You promised you'd try,' Kat implored.

'Okay, fine.'

Max Sherrington reluctantly followed his best friend, Pete, into the bar. God knew he'd rather not be drowning his sorrows in a public place. He had a nice bottle of aged Scotch at home a client had given him that he'd been saving specifically for this day.

The day of the yellow legal envelope.

There was nothing like twenty-year-old whisky to soothe the tension in a man's shoulders and dull the ache in his chest.

But Pete had insisted. And Max knew that when Pete insisted he rarely took no for an answer. He also knew his friend only had his best interests at heart. Pete had been worried about Max and his antisocial behaviour for the last eighteen months.

Max figured, on this day especially, he could give Pete a little of his time.

He had no doubt his friend, a chick magnet if ever there was one, would pick up within the hour and then he would be free to go home to an empty house and a full bottle.

'Right, I'll get the first round,' Pete said, his eyes swivelling the length and breadth of the bar, his gaze coming to rest on a blonde in a red dress whose legs went all the way up to her armpits.

And look at that—she had a friend.

He smiled and tapped Max on the chest. 'I think I see the answer to all your problems.'

Max followed Pete's gaze and almost groaned out loud. 'Why on earth would I want a Tori clone? I thought I was here to exorcise my wife.'

'Ex-wife, bud. Ex,' Pete pointed out.

Ex. That was right. The papers today made it official. He really was going to have to start thinking of her in the past tense.

'Ex,' he said grimly.

Pete slapped him on the back. 'Relax, the blonde's mine. The cute friend is yours.'

Max looked at the other woman. She had a nice face, large eyes, a little snub nose and a bow mouth. Compared to the artfully made-up blonde, she was quite understated. No make-up save some glossy stuff on her lips, no jewellery, no fuss.

But then there was the hair. A riot of short corkscrew curls, the kind that you couldn't get at the hairdresser, sprung from her head. They spiralled like spun sugar and reminded him of butterscotch. An errant one flopped down to brush her eyelashes, which she absently blew away as she swished a straw in her glass.

It was difficult not to notice she also had a great rack.

And looked about as impressed to be here as he did.

'Cute? What the hell am I going to do with cute?' he demanded as an image of peeling her bra aside slid unbidden into his brain. It annoyed him further. 'I don't need cute,' he grouched.

'If you ask me—' Pete grinned '—cute is exactly what you need.'

'I'm doing fine,' he insisted.

Pete gave his friend an exasperated look. 'No. You're not. You've been like a bear with a sore head for the last year and a half. You work twelve- and fifteen-hour days, you've been through five PAs and the only thing you have to break your killer work schedule is a punishing training regime for your next bloody marathon. Oh, and you haven't had sex since Tori left.'

Max grimaced. 'I should never have told you that.'

Pete looked into his best friend's shut-off gaze. He shook his head. 'You really need to get laid.'

Max felt his neck muscles tighten further. If he never got involved with another woman, it would be too soon. Celibacy had been working just fine for him.

He shot his friend a grim look. 'You do know that going without doesn't *actually* kill you, right?'

Pete looked at the shell of a man before him. He'd never met a zombie but Max was doing a fairly good impression. 'I would dispute that.'

Pete glanced back at the blonde, pleased to see she'd spotted him. He smiled at her and she flashed him a dazzler of her own. He turned back to Max. 'Go and find us somewhere to sit, and remember—when I bring these women over do not tell them you're a lawyer. People don't like lawyers.'

Max gave his friend a belligerent stare. That was easy to say when you had them on tap. 'They do if they ever get in trouble with the law.'

Pete sighed. 'Not so much then either, buddy.'

Half an hour had passed since Ali had sent Mr Nice packing and things hadn't got any better.

No matter how hard she tried to be cool about picking up men in a bar or going home with a stranger—it just wasn't her.

'Oh my God, hottie approaching ten o'clock,' Kat murmured. 'He has a friend too.'

Ali glanced in the indicated direction. Yep. He was a hottie. If you were into overt good looks. Having learned the hard way that there was often not a lot of substance behind a pretty face, she wasn't as thrilled as Kat.

She couldn't see his friend. Not that it mattered. She downed the dregs of her third daiquiri. 'Sorry, Kitty Kat, but I'm done. This just isn't working for me.'

'No, wait,' Kat said, grabbing Ali's hand as it reached for her bag. 'Okay, fine, don't have moving-on sex, go home to the apartment and wallow if you want. Just give me another half an hour.'

Kat glanced up at the rapidly approaching man and Ali followed suit. 'I want that guy,' she said. 'So help a girl out. Just stay for a while, occupy his friend for a bit. I don't want him to feel like a third wheel. This guy could be *the one*. I don't want to put his friends off-side from the get-go.'

Ali rolled her eyes. For as long as she'd known Katarina she'd been searching for *the one*. God knew she'd been through enough men in this crazy pursuit. She looked at the pleading in her friend's ridiculously blue eyes. She guessed it wouldn't kill her to stay a little longer…

Especially if Kat's focus was on seducing herself a man rather than finding one for Ali to seduce. She knew how this game went—she'd certainly played it often enough. She knew her role and she knew when to get lost.

'Okay. Thirty minutes.'

Kat winked. 'That's all I need.'

Pete ushered Ali and Kat over to the low table Max had scored. Four padded seats that looked remarkably like footstools were placed evenly around the table.

'This is Kat and Ali,' Pete announced to Max, holding Kat's hand as she lowered herself onto a stool.

Ali rolled her eyes as she sat herself down unaided.

'And this is Max.'

'Hi, Max,' Kat said brightly.

Ali gave an uninterested nod as she stared into her glass and rode the buzz from her fourth daiquiri. It was probably time to stop now.

Max inclined his head politely. 'Ladies.'

The smooth deep baritone of his voice washed over her like a slow sexy saxophone note and pulled Ali out of the buzz even as it added more bubbles to her blood. She looked up despite herself.

Into two very compelling grey eyes heavily fringed by dark brown lashes. She blinked, surprised by their intensity. By the sadness that lurked in them. By the time she'd widened her gaze to take in all of him a few seconds later, those eyes had totally sucked her in.

She knew all about eyes like that. Had seen them in the mirror every morning for the last year.

'So,' Pete said, indicating the daiquiri glasses. 'Are you ladies celebrating something tonight?'

'More like commiserating.' Kat grinned and put her arm around Ali's shoulder. 'Ali's ratfink ex married his trollop an hour ago and I brought her here to get resoundingly drunk.'

'Ah, well done.' Pete smiled, holding up his beer bottle and clinking it with Ali's glass. 'It's the Australian way, after all. Our forefathers would be very proud.'

'Well,' Kat said, crossing her legs and circling her ankle, 'she ruled out my first option.'

'Oh?' Pete asked, mesmerised by the slow rotation of a fire-engine-red stiletto. 'What was that?'

'Voodoo doll.'

Max almost choked on his beer as Pete threw back his head and laughed. Max raised an eyebrow at the woman who had been thrust upon him. Pete had been right—she was cute with her little snub nose and that persistently floppy curl.

It was a shame her olive gaze was so damn serious—it counteracted the cute very effectively. Max would have to be blind not to see the *keep out* signs.

'Voodoo doll?' Max queried.

Ali temporarily lost her train of thought with the combination of his sad eyes and jazz-band voice. Add to that his classic bone structure—pronounced cheekbones, wide jaw—and full mouth bracketed by interesting indents that she guessed were probably dimples were he ever to exercise them, it was hard to find again.

An interesting three-day growth peppered his jaw. It would have looked designer on Pete but the way Max rubbed at it, a little absently, a little harried, added to his jaded appeal.

'Kat enjoys being dramatic.' She shrugged, picking up the thread.

'What a coincidence,' Max said dryly as he glanced at Pete. He looked back at Ali and rolled his eyes. Her mouth twitched into a small smile and he found himself intrigued despite himself.

Pete ignored his friend. 'I like it. Maybe we could have done the same for you, Max?' Pete leaned in close to Kat. 'Max's divorce was final today.'

Ali watched as Max's gaze, which had glinted with humour just seconds ago, grew suddenly bleak again and it stopped the breath in her lungs. He looked as if he'd had his soul sucked out.

And didn't she know how that felt?

'I'm sorry,' she murmured.

Max looked directly at her. For a moment he felt a bizarre connection with her, a recognition of a fellow human being in misery. Ali had obviously had it rough too.

He shrugged. *'C'est la vie.'*

Silence fell between the four of them for a moment or two before Pete dived back in. 'So, Ali, what do you do?'

Ali dragged her gaze from Max to Pete. Not that Pete was even looking at her. She fought the urge to smile. She had to give the man his due—Pete was doing his damnedest to play the charming host. But she didn't for one moment think Pete gave a rat's arse what she did.

She slid a sidelong glance at Kat who had tensed. 'I'm a b—

'Barista,' Kat finished.

Ali blinked, not comfortable with her promotion from humble coffee-shop girl to barista. And certainly still not comfortable with the chain of events that had led to her current state of employment.

Even though she loved the simplicity, the freedom of it. Even though it appealed immensely as an alternate career path.

'Oh, whereabouts? Max and I are often looking for good coffee.'

Ali cleared the emotion from her throat. 'The River Breeze, at Southbank. It's Kat's place.'

A five-minute conversation followed on the merits of different coffees. It required very little input from Ali and Max.

'That's excellent,' Pete murmured. 'We'll have to drop by, won't we, Max?'

Max slid his friend a patient look. 'Why yes, Pete, we will.'

Ali suppressed a smile. It was obvious Max wanted to be a party to this as much as she did. He looked as if he'd come straight from work, his teal and grey striped tie loosened, his top button undone.

Well, why didn't they just speed it up? Pete and Kat could barely keep their eyes off each other—why drag it out? Get the regulation chit chat out of the way so she and Max could both leave and tomorrow their friends could justify jumping into bed together at such short acquaintance.

'And what do you do, Max?' she asked politely.

Pete, who was smiling at Kat, jumped in quickly. *Too quickly.* 'He's an accountant.'

Ali looked from Max to Pete and back to Max again. 'You're not an accountant, are you?'

Max felt himself smile. It wasn't something he'd done a lot of lately. It felt foreign so he stopped. 'No,' he said dryly, ignoring Pete's eye roll.

Ali felt the full impact of that brief smile. His dimples became defined and deepened. His grey eyes seemed less bleak. She had to wonder how he'd look in full blown belly laughter. 'So, what do you really do?'

'I'm a lawyer.'

Ali's first instinct was to flee. After all, Tom was a lawyer. Not to mention she was going to spend the next who knew how long—months probably—with a lawyer. A very, very good one apparently.

The best.

Still…

The desire to flee was overwhelming and she pushed up off her chair reflexively. Kat caught her wrist and held tight before Ali even had the chance to lift her backside.

Max ran the back of his knuckles along his jaw, taking time to process Ali's surprising re-action. 'You either don't like lawyers or you're a fugitive.'

Kat laughed. 'And they say I'm dramatic. Ratfink ex is a lawyer,' she explained.

It was an explanation that seemed to satisfy Pete, Max noted. But then Pete had ceased thinking with his head the second he'd laid eyes on Kat.

Max, on the other hand, wasn't so sure.

'I'll get us some more drinks,' Pete said.

Kat jumped up. 'I'll come with you.'

Before either Max or Ali could say no to another the lovebirds were halfway to the bar, Pete's arm firmly wrapped around Kat's waist.

And then they were two.

CHAPTER TWO

MAX returned his gaze to Ali, who was looking ready to bolt again. 'You're not really a barista, are you?'

Ali huffed out a breath. 'No. I just work in Kat's coffee shop.'

Which was the truth. Or a semblance of it anyway. She did work at the River Breeze.

Now.

Come Monday she was going to spend an awful lot of time talking to her *very, very* good lawyer about what she'd done before that and she had no desire for a preview.

And besides, that part of her life was over.

Max watched Ali fiddle with her straw. She seemed tense and drawn. There was obviously more of a story there. But even more obviously she didn't want to talk about it.

Which suited him just fine.

He glanced over at the bar where Pete was charming Kat. He looked back at Ali. 'So,' he said, trying to lighten the mood. 'I'm a little out of practice with this. Should I be asking you your star sign or something?' He even forced a smile to his lips.

Ali glanced at him, startled to think he might actually be serious. His self-deprecating grin allayed that fear immediately even as it did funny things to her pulse. She gave a half-laugh. It was a relief to talk to him without Kat hovering. Without expectations. Knowing that he was also no longer trying to appease his friend.

'Something like that, I suppose. I think if you really wanted to impress me, though, you'd try and guess.'

Max liked the sound of her voice. It was evenly modulated. A voice for radio. Or for soothing frightened animals. He smiled and played along. 'Hmm, let me see,' he said, rubbing at his jaw. 'Virgo.'

Ali raised an eyebrow. She knew zip about the zodiac but she could play along. 'Interesting,' she murmured. 'And what makes you think that?'

Now he was stuck. Max didn't have the faintest idea. He'd obviously been out of the game too long. He shrugged and then grinned. Hadn't he seen the Virgo symbol often depicted as a curly-haired chick? With large breasts?

'Because you're a woman?'

Ali held her breath as his dimples lit up. It

didn't hurt that he'd noticed she was a woman either. 'Is that an answer or a question?'

Max frowned. 'I'm sorry?'

'You don't seem too sure about me being a woman.'

'Oh no, sorry.' Max let his gaze drop briefly to the barest hint of cleavage he'd been ignoring since she'd sat opposite. She had some kind of a silky blouse on, which glided interestingly across her chest with the slightest movement.

He returned his eyes to her face. 'I'm very sure about that.'

Ali blushed. Actually blushed. She could feel her nipples tighten in blatant response to his appraisal and she blushed some more.

Max laughed as her cheeks grew a very cute shade of pink. 'So did I guess right?'

Ali struggled to clear her head and act cool, as if good-looking men bantered with her every day. She shook her head. 'Libran, I'm afraid.'

Max snapped his fingers. 'That was my next guess.'

Ali laughed. 'Right.'

Max took a swig of his beer, watching her as he tilted his head back. She'd relaxed a little. They both had. 'Your turn.'

Ali cleared her throat, her gaze fixed on the tanned column of his neck as she absently swished her straw through her drink. Then, when she realised she was staring, she narrowed her eyes and fixed him with a speculative glance.

She knew already of course—it was a no brainer. It had to be Sagittarius. She could picture him stripped to the waist, all planes and muscles, a bow pulled taut, his torso powerful but leashed, ready for action.

Ali swallowed. Was it legal to have such indecent thoughts about a total stranger? Maybe she could ask him for his legal opinion?

Right—as if she could pull off such an obvious flirt.

The sad fact was she just hadn't been born with the flirt gene. 'Pisces.'

Max sucked in a breath. Something had been going on behind those serious eyes. Her pupils had dilated and they'd gone almost khaki they'd darkened so much. It took a moment for her words to sink in. Then he laughed.

Ali frowned. 'What?'

Max grinned. 'A fish? You think I'm a fish?'

Ali smiled back. Those dimples were really something. And when that smile went all the way to his eyes, it was truly something as well. 'Fish are…cute,' she said.

'They're cold and slimy and scaly. Seriously,' he mocked, 'do I seem any of those?'

No, he didn't. She'd bet his skin was warm and smooth and that his mouth was hot and sweet. Ali felt her smile shorten as her brain wandered into dangerous territory. They held each other's gaze and his shortened too as if they'd both remembered simultaneously that this was just pretend flirting.

For show. For the sake of their friends.

Some music started up loudly behind them and Max was pleased for the interruption. He looked at his watch then leaned in closer to be heard. A whiff of rum and strawberries made him want to move closer. 'How much longer do you think we need to stick around for?' He indicated the approaching lovebirds. 'I think we're just in the way now, don't you?'

Ali concurred. 'Most definitely.'

Pete and Kat arrived back to the table carrying more drinks. 'Here we are,' Kat announced, placing them on the table as she sat.

Ali looked at the fifth daiquiri and her stomach rebelled. The four previous ones had well and truly hit their mark and she knew another would not be kind to her head in the morning.

'Ah, no, thanks,' she said, pushing the offered drink aside. She risked a brief glance at Max, who nodded slightly and she stood. 'I'm done in. I'm going to go home.'

'Oh no!' Kat implored, standing also. 'Just a little longer.'

'It's okay, you stay. I'll get a taxi home.'

'No, Ali, I can't let you get a cab home by yourself.'

Max, taking his cue, rose to his feet as well. 'It's okay, I'll see she gets home safely. We can share a cab.'

Ali looked at him, surprised. This, she hadn't expected. Didn't need. 'No, really, it's okay. I'm a big girl—I can get a taxi all by myself.'

Max smiled. 'I don't mind. Really.'

His dimples, appearing suddenly again, were her undoing. She knew he wanted out of this mating ritual as much as she did and she felt like a co-conspirator. She just hoped they weren't being too obvious in their rush to get away.

'Okay…sure.' They could always part ways once they were out of sight.

'Well, I suppose, if you really think it would be all right…' Kat murmured, looking at Pete and then back at her friend, hope and gratitude blazing in her eyes.

Ali nodded. 'Can I have a word first?'

Kat grinned, knowing what was coming. 'Yes, Mother.'

Ali dragged her friend to the side slightly. It was pointless telling Kat not to sleep with Pete. Blind Freddy could see that was where the night was heading. But she couldn't walk away without knowing that her best friend was going to be safe.

'Have you got condoms?' she asked Kat.

'Yes. Would you like some?' Kat teased.

'Some? Bloody hell, how many have you got?'

Kat shrugged. 'It's a big bag. I like to be prepared. I can spare a few.'

A few? Ali blinked. Of course. Regular Girl Scout was her Kat. 'I'm catching a taxi with him, Katarina.' Or pretending to anyway. 'I am not sleeping with him.'

Kat shook her head in dismay. 'He really is very attractive, you know.'

Ali didn't need her friend to tell her that. Everyone in the bar could see that. But even worse than his good looks was his wounded air. Somehow that appealed even more. She knew, without it ever being spoken, he understood how deeply relationships could wound. And that was way more dangerous.

She pursed her lips about to say something then Kat whispered, 'Moving-on sex,' before squeezing Ali's hand and walking back to Pete.

'Are you ready?' Max asked.

Ali flicked her gaze to Kat who winked at her. 'Sure.'

A minute later they were heading out of the doors.

'They didn't exactly protest too much,' Max said, his hand still at her elbow. She was wearing a floaty black skirt and he liked how it swung around her legs and seemed to skim in all the right places.

Ali laughed, feeling lighter now her escape was at hand. Or maybe it was the way her whole arm was warm from his touch or that her side tingled from the accidental contact of their bodies as the crowded confines of the bar had forced them closer.

He released her arm once they were outside in the comparably empty street. Ali stuck out her hand. 'It was nice meeting you, Max. Thanks for making that whole friend set-up thing less awkward.'

Max shrugged and ignored her hand. 'There's a taxi rank just around the corner?'

'Oh no,' she said quickly, dropping her hand. 'You don't have to do that. It's okay, really. They can't see us now,' she joked.

He shrugged again. 'I have to get a taxi home. You have to get a taxi home. It makes sense.'

Their gazes caught and locked for a moment. His was all serious again, grey and solemn, his brow furrowed. She longed to see his dimples one more time and was surprised by the urge to lift her finger and trace the indentations either side of his mouth.

'Okay,' she acquiesced before she did something really dumb like follow through on that impulse.

Unfortunately the queue was staggeringly long for so early in the night and Ali almost groaned. Yes, they'd had a bit of banter going at the bar, but now, with their friends nowhere in sight and no real need to talk to each other, would it be horrendously awkward?

They joined the queue and stood silently for the first minute. Ali felt each second tick by like a bloody great doomsday clock. The movement of the crowd jostled her against him and her nose brushed against a cotton clad pectoral. She apologised and pulled away. But not before she'd inhaled a goodly dose of him.

Boy, oh, boy! He smelled like pheromone-laced chocolate. 'Sorry about the fish thing,' she said, her scrambled brain snatching at the first disjointed thought that passed by.

Max bestowed her with a half-smile as he cupped her elbow to steady her. 'I'm sure my ego can stand it.'

Ali returned his smile. He didn't look like a man whose ego was easily dented. 'So what *is* your sign? Really?'

He rolled his eyes. 'Sagittarius.'

Ali bit her lip as the image from earlier returned with full force, enhanced further by his intoxicating scent. Despite the suit she had no trouble imagining him as the famed archer. Half beast, half man.

All animal.

Max watched her eyes darken again and his gaze was drawn to where her teeth dug into the fullness of her lip. His stomach clenched and his hand tightened on her arm a fraction. 'What?'

Ali shook her head, trying to dispel the image. 'Nothing…it's nothing,' she said and dropped her gaze to the hollow in his throat.

Hair sprung from her head as he looked down on her crown but she hadn't been fast enough to hide the rise of colour in her cheeks. 'You blush easily,' he murmured.

Ali clamped her eyes shut as more heat suffused her face. 'Yes,' she said, then risked a glance at him. 'Sorry.'

Max shook his head. It was refreshing to meet anyone who could still blush these days. It didn't happen often in his line of work and it did tend to colour his world view.

'Don't be,' he said. 'It's…' he made a show of searching for the right word, then smiled at her '…cute.'

Cute? She was never going to hear the end of that one, was she?

She opened her mouth to say so but he was looking at her with those solemn, sad eyes, his smile not quite reaching them. And the heat at her elbow was radiating to her fingers. And the jostle of the line kept pressing them together, creating more heat wherever they touched. And his scent filled her nostrils. Invaded her brain.

And she felt more like a woman right now than she'd felt for an entire year. *Maybe ever felt.*

Ali could feel herself melting on the inside.

And she totally lost her train of thought.

It was crazy. She'd known the man for two seconds. Yet here she was liquefying into a puddle at his feet because he had sad eyes and looked at her as if she was a woman.

She shook her head as Kat's treacherous voice murmured *moving-on sex* in her head.

Ali cleared her throat, determined to pick up the thread of her last coherent thought. 'You're not going to let me forget the Pisces thing, are you?'

Max chuckled. 'Not a chance.'

The queue moved forward and it seemed only gentlemanly to Max to slide his hand to the small of her back and usher her along. Still his fingers tingled and he rubbed them absently against her blouse to erase it.

'Nearly there,' he murmured as the front of the queue came into sight.

Ali swallowed as Max's fingertips seared through the fabric of her shirt and set fire to every cell in their vicinity. She shut her eyes briefly as her nipples beaded against her bra and long forgotten muscles deep inside her trembled.

God, this was insane!

Was it possible to orgasm through a completely non-sexual touch to an area far away from the usual erogenous zones?

With a stranger?

In public?

She squeezed her thighs together, shifting back slightly, and was thankful when his hand dropped away.

Ten minutes later they were about five groups away from the head of the queue when they were given the chance to jump it to complete the numbers for a share cab. Max raised an eyebrow at her and Ali leapt at the chance to shorten the agonising experience of constantly being bumped against him.

His warmth was way too compelling.

His voice way too smooth.

And he smelled way too male.

It was not her intention to do anything other than go home but her libido seemed to have roared to life tonight and she wanted to get out of his orbit pronto.

Just in case.

Her life was complicated enough.

Max grimaced as Ali's body was jammed against him by the third person climbing into the back seat. He could smell the alcohol on the other passenger and he turned slightly, his arm along the back of the bench seat shielding Ali from the worst of it.

It did however push them even closer together and he was excruciatingly aware of her breast squashed against his ribcage, her thigh pressed along the length of his, her curls springing against his jaw, tickling his neck.

It won't be long. It probably won't kill me.

And then she shifted, her fingernails accidentally scraping against his thigh, and the sensation travelled all the way to his groin and inside his underpants. He went very still as his arousal intensified.

What the hell was happening to him tonight? He hadn't thought about being with another woman for over a year and now he was acting like a teenager on a first date. Every move, every breath, every whiff of her perfume headed directly south.

Maybe it was as Pete said. Maybe he did need to get laid.

But not her. Definitely not her. He had enough baggage of his own without picking up hers too. Maybe when he got home he'd go find his little black book.

Dust off the cobwebs…

Because he definitely *was not* going to ask

her to come up for a coffee. He *was not* going to kiss her. And he *was not* going to sleep with her.

Ali had complicated written all over her.

And then she turned her olive-green eyes on him and gave him a small smile. 'Thanks so much, for tonight,' she murmured. 'For rescuing me from the Kat-and-Pete show and distracting me from a day I didn't want to have to think about.'

Max swallowed. Her mouth was so close, it would be too easy to move his in closer...

'I think we rescued each other,' he said, returning her small smile. 'We both needed a laugh. I had a good night too. Better than I'd expected.'

Ali nodded. It was nice to know she'd helped him too. It gave her something else to ponder other than the trip of her pulse and the scorching heat of his body against hers.

Despite that, however, Ali also felt overwhelmingly tired. How she could be in such a heightened state of awareness and simultaneously sleepy wasn't a conundrum her brain cells were up to. She could only assume four daiquiris had something to do with it. It was certainly their usual effect.

She yawned loudly. 'Sorry,' she apologised.

Max smiled. She blinked at him slowly

through heavy-lidded eyes and he felt another fiery dart to his groin.

'It's fine,' he dismissed. 'Lay your head on my shoulder. Go to sleep.'

At least then she wouldn't wiggle so much. *Hopefully.*

Ali opened her mouth to protest but the very small part of her that wasn't utterly turned on was so very tired and somehow she felt safe here next to him with his heat and the daiquiris and the rock of the cab lulling her.

What could it hurt to drop her head against his very inviting shoulder? To sigh as he shifted to make her more comfortable? Place her hand across his chest, burrow it beneath his jacket lapel, feel the scrape of cool satin lining as she snuggled in closer?

'Ali? Ali?'

Ali murmured as the low sexy notes of a saxophone disturbed her pleasant slumber. The smell of man surrounded her and it had been long—so long—since she'd been held that she pushed her face closer to the source. The warm cushion beneath her cheek was fragrant, a steady boom soothing her into a state of bliss.

'Ali?'

The voice was more insistent this time and she fluttered her eyes open, shifting to look up towards the source of the rumbling beneath her ear. It took a few seconds for the world to come into focus. For the steady grey gaze to register, the purr of an engine, the glare of an internal light.

Max smiled as the woman he barely knew bathed him with her sleepy olive gaze. He hadn't felt remotely like moving away from her when they'd got rid of their other back seat passenger and had decided it wasn't right to disturb her.

Besides she'd been warm and soft and smelled like woman and as agonising as it had been he'd forgotten how good it felt to have curves and perfume pressed against him.

'Hey, sleepy head. This is my stop.'

'Sorry.' She smiled back but didn't move. She couldn't. She was utterly reluctant to leave this strange cocoon that balanced on a precipice between platonic and promise.

There was something about his smile. Ali had got the impression from the beginning that he didn't smile much. Or certainly hadn't had much reason to since his marriage had crashed and burned. And God knew she got that. The slightly wounded air about him had loaned him a tragic edge that had tugged at her heartstrings back in the bar.

But right now his smile was tugging in other places and she couldn't deny they'd made a connection tonight, no matter how reluctantly.

Their proximity and the glow from the internal light gave her a close-up she hadn't had as yet. She noticed for the first time his brown hair was lightly streaked with grey. It gave him a bucketload more virility and in that hazy half-world between sleep and arousal it seemed only natural to move her hand up to stroke his matching stubble.

And natural too, to follow with her mouth, pressing it briefly against his. And even though his lips didn't react she felt the thunder in his chest beneath her hand and saw his pupils dilate.

Max shut his eyes and felt all his earlier resolve disappear. 'Do you want to come up?'

Ali nodded.

Hell, yes!

CHAPTER THREE

BETWEEN the taxi, the lift and his apartment door, Ali was having second thoughts. 'I don't usually do this.'

Max paused, the key in his hand hovering near the lock. He could hear the tremor in her voice, see the way she wasn't quite meeting his eye. It was curiously touching.

He dropped his hand. 'If it's any consolation, I don't either.'

Ali glanced at him, surprised at the genuine note of sincerity in his voice.

'There's been no one since my wife left.' He grimaced and corrected himself. 'My ex-wife.'

Their eyes locked and held. She caught a glimpse of his unhappiness again, a swirl of misery in his open honest gaze.

'We don't have to do this,' he murmured. 'We can get in my car and I can take you home.'

His voice stroked her skin in all the right places and she could feel her nipples tighten.

She could go home—he was obviously a gentleman. Or she could go through his door.

And feel like a woman again. Attractive, wanted, desired.

She pulled her bottom lip between her teeth. 'Does it make me a bad person if I want to stay?'

Max smiled. She *was* very, very cute—all puzzled and indecisive. Wanting to and yet not. They were close, so close and the mix of her perfume and almost maidenly hesitancy was a potent combination.

She was staring at his top button. He placed a finger beneath her chin and lifted her face until she was looking straight at him.

'It makes you even more desirable,' he said, his voice husky. And he followed it up with a swift hard kiss, catching her sigh as he pulled away.

Ali stumbled against him slightly, reaching for him as she reeled from his cataclysmic five-second, closed-mouthed lip-lock. How on earth would she survive anything more lingering?

Desirable. He'd said desirable.

She looked up at him shyly, heart hammering, aware suddenly that her hand had bunched up his shirt. She smoothed it automatically as he looked at her expectantly.

Waiting.

She cleared her throat, afraid he might well have kissed her voice away. 'Wow.'

Max gave a half-smile. 'Indeed.' Her bow mouth was parted and she had a kind of stunned look on her face and he had to admit to wanting to see that look again.

Preferably with her clothes off.

'There's more where that came from,' he murmured.

Ali responded to the gentle tease in his tone and his weary smile. It made her want to soothe his brow and let him get lost in her body at the same time.

She held her breath and jumped in. 'Better open the door then.'

It might be crazy but maybe, tonight, crazy was just what she needed.

Max inclined his head before turning to put the key in the lock. He twisted it and shoved the door open. He glanced back at her and gestured for her to precede him.

Oh God, oh God, oh God.

This was really going to happen. Her pulse thrummed a little faster, her breath hitched a little higher. She took a step and faltered, her mind racing ahead, mentally preparing.

'Wait.'

Max dropped his hand and raised an eyebrow. 'Yes?'

'What about…do you have condoms?'

She might be practically vibrating with sexual need but having already interrogated Kat it would be hypocritical to not take charge of her own situation. The doctor in her had seen too many women duped into having unprotected sex by men who were prepared to lie to them to get it.

She knew it was a lot harder to say no when you were almost at the point of no return.

Max blinked at the unexpected question. *Did he?* They hadn't used condoms in their marriage... Wait, yes, he did. Pete had bought him a box shortly after Tori had left and shoved it in Max's bedside-table drawer but not before he'd slipped two into Max's wallet.

Neither supply had been touched.

Max leaned against the doorjamb and grinned at her suddenly fierce-looking face. 'Yes. An entire box.'

Ali ignored the light teasing note in his voice. 'Sexual health is no laughing matter.'

Max attempted a sombre nod. 'I agree.'

Ali couldn't stop the smile that tugged at her mouth. 'I suppose you think I'm being ridiculous?'

Max shook his head. He pushed away from the doorjamb and held out his hand. 'I think you're cute. Very cute.'

'Great, more with the cute,' she grumbled.

But her pulse skipped madly and she didn't

hesitate a moment longer. The tingle as his fingers folded over hers streaked heat up her arm, confirming the rightness of it all.

Max stepped backwards, tugging her gently forward, over the threshold of his apartment. Then inside. Shutting the door with a careless shove, he shrugged out of his jacket and pulled off his tie, his gaze firmly fixed to her softly parted lips.

He crowded in close to her, backing her up until she bumped against the door. Her perfume seemed to thicken as the heat between them intensified. He could hear her breath shorten and knew his had followed suit. His whole body had tightened in anticipation.

Everything was tense.

Everything was hard.

Everywhere.

He placed a hand either side of her head and watched her watch him. Watched her olive eyes darken a shade or two as he picked up that errant curl, stretched it out and let it go.

It sprang back, flopping once again across her eye.

'Cute curl,' he said, dropping a kiss on her eyebrow, the curl brushing his lips.

He ran his index finger down the straight neat line of her nose to where it tilted up slightly at the end. 'Cute nose.' And he dropped a kiss there too.

He moved his palm down to cup her jaw, tracing the outline of her lips, feeling it right down to his groin as they parted on a soft whimper. 'Very. Cute. Mouth,' he whispered.

Ali waited for the inevitable kiss, practically drowning in a fog of desire. She felt as if he'd been stroking her insides instead of dropping chaste kisses, nibbling around her edges. And she needed more. It was as if he'd drugged her and she was craving that next hit.

Max took his time stroking her lips, sweeping his thumb across the glossy cushions. Her breath was warm against the pad of his thumb, the beat of her pulse was wild beneath his palm and her throat moved convulsively as she swallowed. Each sweep intensified his longing but he was determined to hold back.

He knew when he let go and kissed her, really kissed her, there would be no holding back.

No more gentle.

No more slowly.

No more easy.

It had been a long time. And his appetite was back.

Ali had reached screaming point. How could a simple brush to her mouth be felt everywhere? How could it bead her nipples to unbearable hardness? How could it undulate through muscles so deep inside she didn't even know she had them until now? How could it pool liquid heat in places that it hadn't even touched?

'Cute, cute, cute,' Max whispered.

Ali groaned. 'Shut up and kiss me properly.'

And then she took matters into her own hands, standing on tippy-toes and dragging his face towards her, closing the maddening distance.

Max inhaled as their lips met, sucking in her heat and her breath and her sweet, sweet perfume and it was like rocket fuel through his already charged bloodstream.

He exploded.

He ground her against the door, pinning her with his mouth and his hands and his hard, hard body. Demanding entrance into her mouth with his tongue and sweeping inside like a conquering general. She tasted like rum and strawberries and his hunger intensified. Angling her head back, he plundered every moist morsel of it.

She moaned beneath his onslaught, clutched his shoulders, pulled him in deeper and he gave her more. His hands slid to her hips, gripping them hard then releasing only to grip them again, pulling her harder, closer, nearer each time. His erection strained against the maddening friction, getting harder, more demanding.

His lips left hers to explore all the soft, sweet

places of her neck and she moaned again. He'd forgotten how soft women were. How they fitted to a man's body, how they yielded against all the hard angles and planes and moulded just right.

Her fingernails dug into his back and she gasped, 'Max,' as he laved the frantic pulse in the hollow of her throat.

He claimed her mouth again revelling in her noises. He'd missed those mysterious womanly noises. The gasps and the whimpers. The little sighs and moans and the desperate, unintelligible urgings that came from deep inside when you hit a sweet spot and they *did-not-want-you-to-stop*.

She opened for him wide, matching the fervour of his mouth with her own and it was a very potent mix. Heady and sexual and dirty.

Good, dirty.

It had been a long, long time since he'd felt this good. Since he'd last kissed a woman he didn't really know. And he'd been more than fine with that. He'd been happily married, perfectly content. But that was then and this was now and Ali was shifting against him with reckless abandon that felt good everywhere.

For the first time in a long time he felt good.

Everywhere.

And he was going to damn well take what was on offer.

Pete had been right. He did need this.

Ali could barely breathe from the lust slugging her system, thickening in her veins like molten lava, beading like liquid mercury. She was dizzy and light-headed but strangely heavy-limbed all at once.

His tongue was stroking against hers— prodding and probing and lapping against her mouth as if it had been crafted especially for him from the world's sweetest chocolate. She could taste beer and opened to him to taste some more.

His hands were clamped on her hips, scorching his palm prints into her flesh like a brand and his groin was pressed so intimately against her she already knew what it was going to feel like to have him inside her.

She'd forgotten how great this was. How kisses could last for hours. How the taste of someone new could be so endlessly fascinating you just couldn't stop. How the need to touch them, taste them, became an overriding imperative. How being intimate with a man could make you feel loose and yet tight in all the right spots.

She realised it was probably the first time in a year she'd gone this long without thinking about Tom.

If this was moving-on sex then she was a convert.

She thrust her hips against his hard belly again and rubbed herself against the even harder ridge that was driving her mad. She wanted to touch it. Feel its steel and its heat and its purpose. Wanted to touch all of him. To see him naked. To press her lips to every inch of his flesh.

To make him moan.

To make him come.

To make him beg for more.

'I need to see you,' Max groaned into her neck as he pulled her blouse out of the waistband of her skirt.

And she knew exactly how he felt. She wanted more. Needed more. More than passionate kisses and fully-clothed fumblings. She needed to see his flesh. Familiarise herself with his skin. Surround herself with the aroma of pure male animal. Inhale the very essence of him.

She followed suit, pulling his shirt-tails out of his trousers and fumbling like a two-year-old with his buttons as he licked heat along her collarbone. It rendered her fingers totally useless and her eyes rolled back as his tongue dipped lower, tracing the full curve of one breast.

How long had it been since a man had taken the time to seduce her so thoroughly? Tom had certainly never been this thorough. And those few teenage fumblings had been exciting at the time but had most definitely lacked the finesse that oozed from Max's fingertips like some kind of sexual magician.

Or was that genius?

A fingertip whispered against her nipple and she almost fainted from the pleasure. She gripped his shirt for fear of falling and moaned her pleasure—again.

His half-opened shirt brought her back to her original mission and she tried again to divest him of it. But as his fingers continued to lightly tease her nipples, stoking her pleasure higher, she gave up the battle, grasped both sides of his shirt and ripped.

A button pinged on the door near their heads and it momentarily shocked them out of their haze. Ali, breathing hard, stared at his bare chest, stunned by both her handiwork and his pure male magnificence.

She blinked. 'I'm…I'm sorry,' she murmured.

Max, breathing even harder, looked down at his tattered shirt. 'I have a dozen more,' he said.

And reclaimed her mouth.

She speared the fingers of one hand into his hair, dragging his head closer as her other hand stroked his chest, his back, his belly. She felt his muscles contract in her wake and broke off the kiss to follow with her mouth. To put her lips where her fingers had been.

She kissed down his neck. Nibbled at his collarbone. Ran her nose across the rounded heat of a perfectly formed pectoral. And swiped her hot tongue across his disc-like nipple.

Ali was sure it sizzled but his loud groan obliterated the soft hiss.

Max could feel his control unravelling as she laved his chest with her tongue. It made him harder and hotter and hungrier than he'd ever been. He didn't want her to stop but he needed more.

He pushed her back. Her face was flushed, her mouth moist from its ministrations and his breath hissed out. 'I want to look at you,' he half groaned, half growled.

Ali sucked in a breath at his guttural command. She was incapable of thinking never mind denying him. Everything felt good and him looking at her could only feel better.

She smiled at him through lust-laden lids. 'Be my guest.'

Max made short work of the buttons on her blouse. Two glorious mounds of soft female flesh greeted him and he just stared for a few moments. She was wearing a see-through bra and he could clearly see her nipples scrunched like perfectly edible berries.

'Max,' she whispered, uncaring of the plea

in her voice as she wantonly arched her back. Didn't he know he couldn't look at her as if he wanted to eat her without following through?

He ran both thumbs down the centre point of each breast, grazing the nipples as he went. Her breath hitched loudly and his erection surged at the strangled whimper that slid from her lips. He reached down into the deep valley between and unsnapped the front clasp. They sprang free—round and full, falling softly into a natural pendulum, the aroused nipples precisely centred.

He filled his hands with her and they spilled over his large palms. He squeezed, brushing his thumbs over the taut buds teasing him with their perfection.

'Max,' she moaned, clutching his head as he bent over them and created exquisite havoc with his tongue.

When he tugged a nipple deep into the heat of his mouth she bucked and cried out, her heel kicking at the door. And he got harder. He slid a hand behind her, between her shoulder blades, pressing her closer still, wanting to taste all of her, to devour all of her.

Her moans, her murmurs, her little strangled sobs were a powerful turn on and he wouldn't stop teasing her until he'd wrung every single one from deep inside her. Tonight was about forgetting but it was also about remembering.

He'd been good at this. And he wanted to be one man that Ali never forgot.

Ali was sure she was drooling. She certainly felt as if she was babbling incoherently. Her breasts had been an erogenous zone that Tom had never really paid attention to. Sure, he'd liked that she had them, that they looked good, that he was the envy of his friends. But he'd virtually ignored them when they'd been making love.

It was a revelation to be with a man who treated them with such reverence. Who was content to worship them as if they were the most perfect set of breasts that ever existed.

She could have been perfectly happily have him do this all night. In fact as his teeth grazed a sensitive peak and her belly contracted she was damn sure after a year of abstinence she could get off on this alone.

But she also needed to explore him. Was hungry to feel the hot, hard length of him. In her hand. Against her belly. Deep inside her.

Summoning the few functioning brain cells she had left, she reached for him. Her hand found her target instantly, thick and straining against the fabric of his trousers. She scraped her nails against him and he lifted his head from her breasts on a groan.

Max looked Ali in the eye as she squeezed him hard. 'Oh, God,' he panted, shutting his eyes at the erotic torture. Ali smiled at him, her face flushed, her olive eyes khaki with undiluted lust.

'Don't stop,' he whispered and lowered his mouth to a peaked nipple and sucked on it hard.

Ali clutched harder, fumbling for the zipper, not wanting to stop but needing more access. Needing to feel the warm silky flesh covering all that hardness. Needing to feel all of him.

Max reared back bellowing loudly when her hand made its first contact. She palmed the length of him and his breath hissed out like a steam engine. She did it again and he moaned deep and low. And when she rolled her thumb across the spongy firmness of his head he cried out.

And then he kissed her. Deep and hard, his tongue thrusting in sync with the motion of his hips as her hands continued to grip him, encircle him.

'I want you in me,' she whispered against his mouth. 'Now!'

Max needed no further encouragement. He reached for her skirt and rucked it up both sides, his hands sliding around to the cheeks of her backside, squeezing tight, urging her closer to him. His hands found the narrow strip of fabric sitting on each hip and figured she was wearing some kind of G-string.

He grabbed one side and yanked, snapping it as if it were dental floss. 'Sorry,' he murmured against her mouth with not one ounce of contrition.

Ali smiled. 'I have a dozen more.'

And then his fingers were stroking her and Ali couldn't have cared less if they were made out of spun gold and were the rarest knickers in the world.

'Condom,' Max said to her as he slid first one finger and then another into her tight moist heat.

'Wallet,' he directed and then claimed her nipple.

Ali's knees buckled and she was grateful when he braced his legs against hers for support. Reluctant to let go of all his magnificent male hardness, she fumbled in his trouser pocket with her other hand. Locating his wallet was easy but getting it out and open while his fingers filled her and rubbed in just the right spot was a task almost beyond her. She could already feel a delicious tightening.

Max lifted his head. 'Hurry,' he growled and turned his attention to the other nipple.

There was no choice. She had to let him go. Still, her hands shook as she located the foil packet and then opened it. The steady rhythm of his fingers moving her inexorably closer to orgasm caused her to fumble as she attempted to roll it on.

'Ali, for God's sake,' Max groaned into her neck.

'I can't…concentrate,' she panted as a ripple undulated through her. 'You…oh…dear God…' she drew in a ragged breath '…that feels so good.'

Max smiled at her lust-drunk expression. It felt good to see that look, to know he'd put it there. 'What, this?' he asked, circling his fingers.

Ali gasped. 'God, yes, please…stop. I'm never going to be able to put this damn thing on otherwise.'

Max acquiesced but kept his hand firmly in place. 'That better?'

Ali shut her eyes as the ripples petered off. 'Marginally.' It was enough to accomplish her goal anyway and it was Max's turn to pale as she created her own brand of havoc sheathing him slowly and thoroughly.

'Ali,' he warned, squeezing his eyes shut, ruthlessly suppressing the urge to rear like a rutting stallion.

It was Ali's turn to smile but she heeded his warning nonetheless, completing the job post-haste. 'Go,' she said, leaning forward and kissing him full and hot and open. 'Now!'

Max didn't have to be asked twice. He slid

his hand down her thigh and urged her leg up. He bent it at the knee and held it close to his waist as he pushed inside her in one easy movement.

Ali gasped, digging her fingers into his shoulder blade. 'Yes.'

Max repeated the movement, sliding higher this time, her gasp mingling with his groan somewhere inside their heated kiss.

Max pushed again and again. The movement rocked her against the door and jiggled her breasts most enticingly. Too enticingly as he switched his attention from her mouth to her still-taut nipples.

Ali whimpered. The delicious push and pull of Max and the erotic swipe of his tongue were all-consuming. She burned, throbbed, ached, yearned. The pressure built and built, the ripples returned and her breathing grew shorter, harder, faster.

Max could feel the ripples too. The sensation started at his belly button and radiated down. Ali's desperate little gasps and the thrum of his own blood strengthened it. His biceps trembled, his shoulders quivered as the sensation raced like a rogue electrical storm through every muscle group.

It finally came to rest down deep and low and grew, expanded, intensified.

'Max!' Ali gasped as her orgasm hit, clutching him close. 'Max, Max, Max!'

He felt her tighten around him, her muscles undulating along his length, milking him, demanding his surrender. His blood tingled. His nerve endings tightened. And when she threw her head back against the door in a silent scream he yielded to the demands of both their bodies, joining her somewhere in the stratosphere, holding tight as starlight rained down on them.

Ali felt heavy as she bumped back down to earth. But curiously weightless. She shifted in Max's arms, aware that he was essentially holding her up.

Max gripped her thigh, not wanting to move, not wanting to spoil a moment that would be with him until the day he died. 'You okay?' he asked.

Ali shook her head. She never knew sex could be completely mind-bending. How had she got to twenty-nine and not known that sex could be this good?

'I doubt I'll ever be okay again. I think I just touched the stars.'

Max smiled. It *had* been pretty incredible. He lifted his head from the hollow of her neck. 'Pretty good for a fish, huh?'

Ali laughed as she traced her fingers through

his stubble. 'Please tell me you can do that again.'

Max chuckled. 'I may need a moment.'

She laughed again, feeling light and loose and free of a year full of baggage—even if only for tonight. 'It'd be such a shame not to put a few more of those condoms to good use. Don't you think?'

Max kissed her neck. 'Absolutely.'

CHAPTER FOUR

ALI was going to throw up.

She couldn't remember ever being this nervous. Not even that time when one of the world's top neurosurgeons with a reputation for being an arrogant jerk had peered over her shoulder during her first ever solo op and demanded she explain the rationale for every single scalpel movement and instrument choice.

Sure, she'd had butterflies—her career had been at stake. But she'd known her stuff. Had been confident in her ability. Surgery she knew. Surgery she could do.

But this?

This was a complete unknown. This was utterly terrifying!

The nervous squall lashing her insides was not helped by the pitch and roll of the taxi. The driver was riding the accelerator like a yo-yo and it took all her skill to keep the cardboard tray with the two take-away coffee cups balanced and upright.

The aroma of Arabica beans infused her nostrils as the liquid sloshed in the cups, intensifying her nausea. Ali was glad she'd made the decision not to put anything into her stomach today. Adding food to this volatile mix of shredded nerves and perpetual motion wouldn't have been pretty on the floor of the cab.

She was never more grateful than when the taxi pulled up in front of the exclusive riverside high-rise. She paid the driver and gingerly stepped out of the cab, her thigh muscles wobbling as she regained her land legs. She craned her neck upwards. The mirrored blue glass cast a mighty shadow over the Brisbane River somehow looking cold and clinical even in the sunshine.

More cold and clinical than an operating theatre ever had!

She forced her legs to move towards the glass sliding doors, her fingers gripping the tray of hot beverages. She entered the building and headed towards the steel and frosted-glass directory, her heels tapping on the glossy Italian-looking marble.

She perused the directory, searching for Messrs Sherrington, Watkins, Appleby and Dawson finding them on the forty-sixth floor. Ali's stomach dipped at the thought.

She entered the lift, pleased to be alone as she juggled the tray and her bag to push the button. Her nerves ratcheted up another ten notches as the lift launched effortlessly to the lofty heights of the penthouse floor. Of course it glided silently, in tip-top shape as she expected everything was in this state-of-the-art building.

She noticed she was biting her bottom lip again as she checked out her reflection in the mirrored back wall and she released the swollen piece of flesh that had been under constant attack all weekend and was now quite tender.

It was hard to believe the terrified looking woman staring back at her was her.

Aleisha Gregory.

Dr Aleisha Gregory she reminded herself.

But not for much longer.

She flicked the usual curl from her eye and fiddled with a lapel to distract her from such defeatist thoughts. She felt strange all suited up like this. The black jacket with a fine burgundy pin-stripe felt odd, as did the matching tailored trousers. The soft burgundy silk of her blouse fell lightly against her skin caressing the fullness of her breasts, not all starched and abrasive like her baggy scrubs when she'd first put them on in the morning.

She'd give anything for those scrubs right now. Or her regulation jeans and T-shirt, but her mother was a great believer that one should *dress* for appointments and, after their phone call this morning, she just couldn't override Cynthia Gregory's voice.

The elevator pinged and the fist that had been shoved up under her diaphragm ground a little deeper. Ali took a deep breath and stepped out into the plush pile of expensive carpet. A gleaming glass door opposite the lift pronounced that she had indeed reached the offices of one Godfrey Sherrington.

She entered the foyer area dominated by a large reception desk constructed from a slab of timber that was heavy, dark and glossy. The rest was fairly regulation—if watching every television law show ever made was any indication. Muted lighting, leather accessories, expensive greenery and even more expensive art.

'Can I help you?'

Ali dragged her gaze off a painting that could easily have hung in the National Gallery and focused on the not-too-young, not-too-old receptionist who somehow blended with the understated elegance of the surroundings.

'Yes, I'm here…' Her voice wobbled and she cleared it. 'I have an appointment with Godfrey Sherrington.'

Her name was enquired after and a phone call was made and then she was directed to the very masculine-looking lounge. 'Mr Sherrington will be with you in a moment.'

Ali sat, the reality of it all suddenly hitting

her. Her legs felt as if she were back in the taxi and she was grateful for the soft leather of the lounge even if it did look as if it belonged in an exclusive men's club.

Or an expensive brothel.

Her gaze fell on a portrait of a kindly-looking grey-haired gent. A plaque at the bottom announced him to be Godfrey Sherrington. Ali felt her spirits rise. He looked just the ticket. Aged. Wise. Scholarly. Experienced with the law.

Hell, even the name Godfrey inspired confidence. It conjured images of several generations of legal men. Well-known and respected barristers, QCs, maybe even a judge or two.

She'd been told by the hospital's CEO he was the best damn medical defence lawyer in the country and looking at this portrait she could believe it.

Godfrey Sherrington looked like a man who could melt an opposing team's argument with a few blistering words and then sit down, pat her hand and assure her everything was going to be okay.

She really hoped so. Because she was going to need a lot of hand patting through this whole ordeal. And it really did help settle her churning stomach to think that Godfrey Sherrington's hand would be soft and wrinkled. Like her grandfather's.

'Mr Sherrington will see you now.'

Ali started, the tray tilting perilously. She stood and followed the efficient receptionist down a hallway to the end door. The woman knocked and opened in one smooth movement. She indicated another set of leather lounge chairs clustered around a low table and said, 'Mr Sherrington won't be a moment.'

Ali, whose heart now beat so loudly she was sure seismologists all over the world were wondering what the hell was going on in Brisbane, watched the woman disappear. She stood in the middle of the palatial room looking the proverbial fish out of water.

Massive glass windows afforded her a million-dollar view of the city skyline and down the river. So this was how the other half lived. Her office at work was a two-by-two shared affair just large enough for a desk, two chairs and a skinny examining table.

She moved towards the windows, feeling less and less comforted by the prospect of a lawyer called Godfrey. This was the big league!

She looked down spying a RiverCat speeding from Eagle St Pier across to Southbank. Her gaze tracked the boat and watched as it disgorged its human cargo. She followed the ant-like movements of the disembarked passengers as they enjoyed a sunny Brisbane morning and would have given anything to be down there with them—not a care in the world.

She followed the meandering path of the riverside walk and suddenly realised she could see the River Breeze. Kat's pride and joy. And her current refuge from a world gone crazy.

Max washed his hands at the vanity and inspected his face. He'd gone with the whole shaggy look when his life had gone pear-shaped and though the style was frowned upon in the ultra-conservative world of law, being one of the principals in a respected law firm, not to mention a top-notch lawyer with a fearsome reputation, gave him a whole lot of latitude.

Certainly his great-great-grandfather Godfrey Sherrington the first would not have approved. But at thirty-five he'd long ago stopped giving a damn what people thought. This last eighteen months particularly.

He dried his hands, then checked his tie was straight. The same tie he'd worn to the bar on Friday night. Henceforth to be for ever known as his lucky tie. He smiled at his reflection. He'd been doing that a lot since Friday.

Pete had called around Saturday night to watch the game with him and had known something was up within minutes.

'Okay,' he'd said. 'What's the matter?'

Max had taken a swig of his beer, his gaze firmly fixed on the television. 'What do you mean?'

Pete's eyes had narrowed. 'You're smiling.'

Max had chuckled. 'Jeez, sorry.'

Pete's eyes had narrowed even further. 'And now you're laughing?' He'd processed it for a second or two. 'Oh my God,' he'd said. 'You got laid, didn't you?'

Max had hidden his next smile by taking another swig from his bottle. 'Are we watching this game or not?'

Pete had tried in vain to dig out the details but Max had always abhorred locker-room talk and had seen the consequences of it played out too many times in courtrooms. He'd refused to confirm or deny anything and Pete had eventually given up.

But even now Friday night was still bringing a smile to his face. It had been incredible. She had been incredible. Generous. Playful. Adventurous. And even if he never saw her again, he knew their night together would go down as one of life's best memories.

Although, he had to admit, seeing her again was a very attractive proposition. Not that he knew anything about her other than her first name. No numbers were exchanged, no promises were given. But he could find her if he wanted to. He had no doubt that Pete was in touch with Kat so finding Ali would be very easy.

But.

They'd both known the score on Friday night. They'd both known they were convenient bodies to get lost in for a little while. To forget for the night.

Still, he couldn't deny the strength of the urge to see her again if only to thank her for helping him to see that there was life and laughter after a decree absolute.

Nah. Who was he kidding? He had a whole box of condoms and he'd like nothing more than using them all up with her.

He shook his head as an image of her lying naked on his bed flashed before him, that damn curl falling in her eye, a Mona Lisa smile playing on her very kissable mouth.

He really needed to stop.

He couldn't be thinking about Ali when another woman waited for him outside. One who was no doubt scared and nervous and worried sick. One who deserved his full, undivided attention.

Dr Aleisha Gregory needed him to have his head in the game. She was relying on him. As was Brisbane Memorial Hospital—one of his, and the firm's, biggest clients.

'Get it together, bud,' he told his reflection before pushing off the sink.

Striding out into his office a moment later, he located the figure by the windows and announced, 'I'm so sorry to have kept you waiting.'

Her back was to him and she was obviously enthralled by the views from the forty-sixth floor. And then her curly butterscotch hair registered and a sudden sense of foreboding descended.

Ali frowned as a familiar voice invaded her turbulent thoughts. She turned. 'Max?'

Max blinked. What the—? His eyes raked her from top to bottom, not quite trusting that he hadn't just conjured her up. Errant curl, sexy mouth, blush spreading across high cheekbones.

It was her all right.

He glanced at the tray in her hands with the two coffee mugs boasting a River Breeze logo. He relaxed. She'd found out through Kat where he worked and decided she'd drop by. Bring some of that coffee Kat had boasted about on Friday night.

Hell, he was all for spontaneity. Especially if it came in such a delectable package. And hadn't he just been thinking he'd like to see her again?

He might not be in the market for a relationship but a little bit more of Friday night he could definitely handle.

He smiled. 'Well, this is a nice surprise,' he murmured, moving forward.

When he stopped in front of her he had absolutely no intention of kissing her. But then her mouth parted slightly and he grasped her lapels, yanked her forward and kissed her with a hunger that he hadn't realised still existed until their lips met.

Ali's gasp was smothered by the ferocity of his expert mouth and for a few seconds she was too stunned to do anything. But a flood of memories from Friday night returned on a rush of hormones.

He smelled better than she remembered. Felt better. If possible, even kissed better.

Ali wasn't sure what was going on and at the moment she didn't care because for the first time all morning she didn't feel in imminent danger of throwing up. For the first time all morning she'd forgotten about the whole stupid mess she was in.

So she melted against his mouth and hung on for dear life. Which was just as well because when he released her just as abruptly a good minute later, she staggered slightly.

Hell, she even whimpered.

'For me?' he asked, taking one of the cups and parking his butt on the deep window sill behind him.

'Er...' she said, straightening and trying

to order rather scattered thoughts. Actually she'd bought it for Godfrey Sherrington but she guessed he could have hers. It probably seemed a silly gesture to a legal god, but Ali had wanted to break the ice, endear herself.

She wanted Godfrey Sherrington to like her. To believe her. Not just because he was defending her and he had to, but because she knew deep in her heart that this mess wasn't her fault and she wanted him to know it too.

'It should be hot enough still,' she said absently. 'I made them scalding just as the taxi pulled up so they should be a good temperature right now.'

She was babbling. She knew that. She needed to stop. But he was so near, his broad shoulders blocking her view, the knot of his tie at her eye level. She'd kissed what lay beneath that knot. Knew what he smelled like there. Had felt that pulse push against her lips.

She dropped her gaze to rid herself of the image only to be mesmerised by his swinging leg. The movement pulled the fabric of his trousers taut across his thigh. A thigh she knew. She'd touched. She'd gripped. Licked.

Gnawed.

She shut her eyes briefly. *Stop it!*

'So,' she said, taking a step back and clearing her voice. She would concentrate on the matter at hand if it killed her. 'I'm sorry, do you work for Godfrey Sherrington? Are you his... understudy?'

She massaged her forehead as she groped for the right terminology. 'Or article clerk? Second chair? I don't know...whatever the hell they call it in legal circles?'

Max frowned. What on earth was she babbling about?

'Because, no offence, but I've heard he's the best and, apart from the obvious conflict of interest here, I really need the best. And, not to put too fine a point on it but I think the hospital expects it too. I really don't want to be palmed off to his...assistant.'

Max straightened, pushing off the window sill, that feeling of foreboding returning.

The hospital expects?

I really need?

Don't want to be palmed off?

He looked straight at her, the woman he'd spent hours and hours in bed with three days before, exploring every inch of her body. The woman whose lip gloss he'd just thoroughly kissed off.

'Ali,' he said quietly. '*I* am Godfrey Sherrington.'

She stared at him blankly. 'But you're Max.' Max whose taste was still on her tongue, whose smell was still on her skin.

Max stalked past her, cramming a hand

through his hair. He stopped at his desk, placed his knuckles on the side and bowed his head. 'You're Aleisha Gregory, aren't you?'

Ali stared at his back as the implication slowly sank in. 'Oh, my, God.'

Max turned and sat on the edge of his desk. 'Indeed.'

The nausea that had threatened all morning suddenly rose and Ali placed a hand over her mouth. 'I'm going to be sick.'

Max knew exactly how she felt. This was a complete disaster! 'Yes,' he replied miserably.

'No,' Ali said urgently, dropping her bag with a thunk and travelling towards him, 'I'm *really* going to be sick.'

Max started at the urgency of her tone and the sudden pallor that had turned her golden complexion white as paper. 'Bathroom through that door.' He pointed.

Ali made it just in time. Not that she had anything to bring up but it didn't stop the waves of retching or the hot tears that spilled over her lids and coursed down her cheeks.

This. Could. Not. Be. Happening.

Had she really spent several sweaty hours rolling around in bed with her lawyer the other night? Her kick-arse, top-notch, take-no-prisoners, best-in-town lawyer?

She groaned. Was nothing ever going to go

right for her ever again? Was she cursed? Had she broken a mirror? Walked under a ladder?

She'd been a good person, hadn't she? She gave to charity. Never cheated on her taxes. Always told checkout staff if she'd been given too much change.

She operated on people's brains, for crying out loud!

Ali dragged herself up to the basin. She looked awful. Her nose was running, she had red eyes, a blotchy neck and two wet tracks running down her cheeks.

It was the only time in her life she wished she wore make-up so she could do a quick repair job. But seriously what would have been the point when she spent eighty per cent of her day behind a surgical mask?

Maybe after all this was over she'd get a job at a department store where she could put on a face every day and do something frivolous like sell handbags.

She loved handbags.

A knock sounded on the door, followed by, 'Ali? Are you okay in there?'

Okay? Did he have any idea how *not* okay her life was? How the one person she'd pinned her hopes on to make it all okay again—her lawyer—turned out to be a man she'd had hot, sweaty, best-sex-of-her-life with not even seventy-two hours ago.

She'd told him then she was never going to be okay again but this was a whole other twist.

'Ali?' Louder this time.

'I...I'm fine,' she called. 'I'll be right out.' There was no point hiding away in here—it wasn't going to make the problem go away.

Ali jerked the tap on and threw water over her face, scrubbing at it with her hands. Then she pulled off some paper towel and dabbed at the moisture, patting herself dry. She gave herself a quick once over in the mirror.

Still awful. But less soggy.

Just as well she hadn't gone and done something really foolish on Friday night like thinking there was something more to their time together other than a sexual tryst. Because the face that stared back at her now was not the face a woman wanted a man to see.

Ali took a deep breath and used an unsteady hand to push the door open. Max, who was standing at the windows, turned when he heard the click.

They looked at each other for a moment or two. 'So,' she said. 'Is Max a name you give to women in bars so they won't laugh at you when you tell them your real name?'

Max would have had to have been deaf to miss the sarcasm. He raised an eyebrow. 'People who live in glass houses shouldn't throw stones, *Ali*.'

She held his gaze, refusing to waver. 'Ali is short for Aleisha,' she snapped.

'And the coffee-shop-girl routine?'

'I *am* a coffee-shop girl. Right now, coffee-shop girl is me.'

Right now coffee-shop girl was looking pretty damn good all round.

Max regarded her silently for a brief moment before wandering back to his desk and throwing himself in his chair. He speared his fingers through his hair again and leaned back into the plush leather.

'My full name is Godfrey Maxwell Sherrington. My father apparently insisted, family tradition et cetera. My mother, who, thank goodness, was a little more sensitive to modern conventions, realised it was an unfortunate name to lumber a seventies child with, acquiesced to this demand only under the proviso that I would be called Max. I've never been called anything other than Max.'

Ali watched the weariness that had so affected her on Friday night cloud his grey eyes again. Damn Max and those eyes. So, he hadn't deliberately misled her—it still didn't erase the fact that two cases of mistaken identity had landed them in a bit of a pickle.

And while her sappy heart, the part of it that sympathised with human misery, wanted her to go easy, the part fighting for her very existence tended to be more bitchy.

'It says Godfrey on the board downstairs, on the glass sliding doors in the foyer and on the door to this office,' she pointed out, ticking each point off on her fingers. 'And I bet if I find a piece of paper,' she said, marching over to his desk and whisking up a blank piece, 'it'll say Godfrey on your personalised stationery.'

She turned it around and pointed to the of-fending letterhead.

Max leaned forward, elbows on his desk, massaging his temples. 'It's my legal name. It's on all documents and signage. Just like Aleisha, no doubt.'

Ali glared down at him, annoyed that he was right and they both knew it. 'Doctors who work in the public health care system don't have sta-tionery,' she said waspishly.

Max looked up at her, olive eyes going that stormy shade of khaki again. He sighed and in-dicated the chair opposite him. 'Sit down, Ali.'

Ali stood frowning at him for a few more moments. He returned her stare without wa-vering and she rolled her eyes. 'Fine,' she said, sinking into the plush leather of the most com-fortable chair she'd ever had the pleasure of sit-ting in.

Well didn't that figure?

Her office chair gave her lumbar pain within a minute of sitting on its hard plastic seat.

In her next job she'd make sure a comfortable chair was written into her contract. An office job with an ergonomically designed chair—now that she could do.

'This is a disaster, isn't it?'

She looked exactly as she had the other night, big olive eyes uncertain, teeth pulling at her bottom lip as she'd asked if wanting to go to bed with him made her a bad person.

He remembered how that mouth had felt against his. How it had trailed all over his body. Stroked down his belly. Stroked lower…

'It figures, really. Pretty much par for the course for my life lately.'

Her words dragged him back from Friday night. Back to the present. For crying out loud—she was right there, in front of him! *Looking like hell.* As if her entire world had just been tipped upside down. And shaken for good measure.

Thinking about Friday night was *not* appropriate.

'Where do we go from here?'

There was finality in her tone that was heartbreaking and he rushed to assure her but she wasn't done with the one-sided conversation.

'Perhaps you can recommend someone else in the firm that could deal with the case?'

Max frowned, not quite keeping up with the leaps she was taking. 'I'm sorry?'

'I assume you'll have to recuse yourself?'

And then to his utter horror her face crumpled and she burst into tears.

CHAPTER FIVE

ALI wanted a hole to open up in Max's very expensive-looking Persian rug and swallow her up. Her heart thunked against her ribs as if a large piece of space junk had just landed smack in the middle of her chest.

This could not be happening.

Was it not bad enough to have slept with him? Did she have to go and add public humiliation to her sins?

'I'm s-sorry,' she snivelled, her nose and eyes streaming as she desperately tried to stem the tears that she'd held at bay for so long now.

Since her suspension.

Since before that—her ex, the baby.

'I don't know what's wrong with me, I n-n-never cry.'

Max knew. He'd read her case file several times. He knew her state of mind was shot. He knew she'd been through a roller-coaster ride of emotion. Of suspension and enquiries and reinstatements and further suspension while the case went to court.

He also now knew her ex had left her for another woman.

And then, to cap it off, she'd gone and slept with her lawyer.

'That'll be why, then,' he said dryly, her kicked-puppy gaze breaking through his well-fortified barriers as he handed her a tissue from the box on his desk.

Ali looked at the snowy white Kleenex in surprise as he waved it at her. He shrugged. 'Occupational hazard.'

'Really?' she asked, taking it, dabbing at her eyes, then blowing her nose.

Well used to being confronted with highly emotional people and situations in her own work environment, she found it a surprise to realise that medicine didn't corner the market on Kleenex usage.

'Sure. Most people come to lawyers when they're in trouble. They're usually pretty emotional.'

She sniffed as the vice gripping her chest eased a little and the last hiccoughy breath died.

'I'm sorry. Please don't think I'm this weak, weepy woman who cries at the slightest hurdle. I've just had...a really bad year.'

'Not at all. If it makes you feel any better

the last person who cried in this office was a hundred-and-fifty-kilo drug dealer who could bench press our combined weight and had spent half of his life in maximum security.'

She smiled despite herself but his calm acceptance of her breakdown depressed her further.

Great.

He was the best. *The* best. Everyone said so. Everyone had assured her that in medical defence law he was *the* lawyer to have.

And she'd screwed it up, royally.

Sure, the charges weren't against her personally, but it was her alleged actions that had caused this whole mess and put the hospital in hot water. It was bad enough Brisbane Memorial had to fight this wrongful death suit—the last thing they needed was to lose their best lawyer because of her too.

The hospital needed a good lawyer. Needed *the* best. And so did she. She had a lot to prove here too.

A lot at stake.

Even if she was never going to pick up a scalpel again, her reputation had been damaged. And that she couldn't live with.

She had to prove her innocence.

And for that she needed the best.

She needed Max.

But now the last few months were wasted.

All that time and money the hospital had ploughed into prepping the case had been sabotaged because of one hot sweaty night between the sheets.

Max looked over at a much more composed Ali. She looked like hell.

He really, really shouldn't want her this bad.

'I don't have to recuse myself.'

Ali sniffled. 'What?'

Max looked at her patiently. 'Ali, we slept together.' Not that there'd been a whole lot of sleeping going on. 'We met for the first time three days ago and slept together with no knowledge of what our relationship was going to be today. There's no law against it.'

Ali felt a moment's hope at his assurance but, given how badly her life had sucked the last year, she wasn't about to dance a jig. Things just hadn't been going her way.

'So…legally, we're fine,' she clarified. 'But what about ethically? Where do we stand there?'

Ali made hard ethical decisions in her job all the time—ethics she understood.

'Ethically I can be disbarred from sleeping with a witness.'

'Oh, God.'

His calm bluntness made her want to throw up again and she gripped the desk to ground herself. It was hard enough living amidst the ruins of her own professional life without feeling responsible for his too.

'If—' he jabbed his index finger at the desk for emphasis '—if, I had prior knowledge. Which I didn't.'

He searched her face. She still looked utterly miserable.

'It's okay, Ali,' he assured her. 'Here are the facts.' He pointed to his index finger. 'We met for the first time as strangers on Friday night. Correct?'

Ali nodded. 'Correct.'

He pointed to his next finger. 'It was a brief one-night stand that meant nothing to either of us other than a fabulous way to forget a miserable day. Correct?'

Ali swallowed as a little part deep inside her mewed in protest. She quashed it ruthlessly. Of course that was all it was—she barely knew the guy!

Just because she'd had the best sex of her life which had possibly ruined her for all other men was immaterial.

'Correct.'

He stabbed at a third finger. 'Unless you're some kind of closet bunny-boiler, which I seriously doubt, we have no intention of pursuing this relationship either during or after the trial. Correct?'

She shook her head emphatically. After the

trial she had to work out what she wanted to do with the rest of her life. Start a new career. There would be no room for all-night-long sexual feasts.

No matter how mind-blowing it had been.

'Correct. Absolutely correct.'

'If, however—' he steepled his fingers '—this is a deal breaker for you, you feel uncomfortable with my representation given...' *how I licked every inch of your body* '...what transpired on Friday night, then, of course, I can recommend several colleagues who can take the case.'

He could practically see the cogs turning in her brain as she chewed on her bottom lip. A lip he'd ravaged more than a little himself...

'But I have to warn you that starting over again with another lead lawyer would necessitate a continuance from the court that could set things back several months. And you need to know that, not only am I fully up to speed with your case, I'm also the best medico-legal lawyer in this city.'

Ali swallowed at the sheer arrogance of his statement. But there wasn't even one brain cell that didn't believe him. He was breathtaking in his total assurance that he was *the* man for the job. Between that and the way he'd calmly and methodically reeled off his points before, she could see how magnificent he'd be in court.

He could certainly hold his own in the arrogance stakes with any consultant surgeon she knew.

And somehow—whether it was his supreme confidence or the connection they'd made the other night—she trusted him.

She certainly didn't want to hang on for another few months. She needed to put this behind her and get on with her life.

Whatever it might hold.

'Okay.' Her voice sounded shallow and breathy and she cleared it. Her mind was made up—she had no time to sound indecisive. 'Okay, then.'

She looked so damn cute trying to conquer her anxiety and be brave with that silly curl flopping in her eye. It reminded him of her anxiety at his door on Friday night, which was the last thing he needed. He quickly cut off that train of thought and clawed back a modicum of professionalism.

'I have to be clear, though, that there is a line drawn between us now that neither of us can cross. We had no control over what happened a few days ago. But we do over what happens from now on.'

Aleisha nodded at his brisk businesslike tone. 'Of course.'

Whatever he said, whatever he wanted. As

long as he continued with the case, she'd follow his demands to the letter.

She rose on shaky feet. 'How about we start over?' She offered her hand. 'Hi. I'm Dr Aleisha Gregory, pleased to meet you.'

Max looked at her, then at her hand, then back to her. He smiled as he stood and took her hand firmly in his and shook. 'Hi. I'm Max Sherrington.'

Ali felt his smile and the warmth of his hand go straight to her belly and she pulled her bottom lip between her teeth.

Max felt it too as his gaze followed the indent of tiny white teeth torturing a lush lip. 'Your lawyer,' he added.

Because God knew the way he wanted to swipe his tongue across that mouth didn't feel remotely lawyerly.

Half an hour later they were ensconced at a window table at Cha Cha Char, one of the many restaurants dotting the river walk area around Eagle Street pier. Max appeared to be a regular and Ali let him order one of their famous Wagyu steaks for her as she was still too keyed up to concentrate.

Too keyed up to eat, really, but her empty stomach was growling in protest and she was starting to feel light-headed. It was time to put something in her belly or soon her hands would be trembling and she wouldn't be able to take in what he was saying.

And she really needed to keep her wits sharp until this ordeal was over.

'Maybe we should have gone to the River Breeze as I first suggested?' Max murmured as he watched Ali play with her cutlery.

Ali looked up sharply. 'What?'

Her curls bounced to the abrupt movement and he remembered how they had felt trailing against his chest. 'You don't seem very comfortable here.'

Ali frowned. 'Oh. No… Here is…fine.'

The very last thing she needed right now was Kat's perennial cheeriness. Plus, she hadn't told her friend about her and Max getting naked and doing the nasty and Kat was too savvy not to take one look at them together and guess.

And then she'd never hear the end of it.

Max suppressed a smile as Ali returned her attention to her nearby fork. 'Kat doesn't know, does she? About us?'

Ali's fingers froze on the tines of the fork. She peeked up at him through her fringe as she chewed on her lip again.

'That you're my lawyer?' she asked, feigning innocence.

Max quirked an eyebrow. 'That we slept together.'

Ali's cheeks grew warm as she shook her

hair back and looked at him fully. 'No.' She sighed. 'Kat's a romantic. Truly, it's best she doesn't know. Especially with this new…development. She'll start talking about destiny and, trust me on this, that's one load of hippy mumbo-jumbo I've heard one too many times.'

Max chuckled. 'You don't believe in destiny?'

Ali looked him square in the eye. 'I believe in hard work and self-determination.'

He nodded. 'Me too.'

There was a pause and Ali realised she'd relaxed a little. She picked up the spoon and absently doodled a pattern on the white tablecloth. 'Does Pete know?'

Max shook his head abruptly. 'I don't kiss and tell.'

Ali blinked at the sudden starch in his voice. 'I didn't think you would.'

Frankly it hadn't occurred to her that Max would be indiscreet. He hadn't struck her as the type. In retrospect that had probably been naïve but it was good to know her instincts had been on the money.

Max relaxed and even managed a small smile. 'Pete thinks he knows. He has a vivid imagination.'

Ali smiled in response. 'I think he and Kat are going to get along famously.'

The waitress arrived with their drinks, interrupting the only sense of shared history they had, and Ali was reminded that they weren't here socially. She took a sip of her diet cola and looked at him.

'So, what do we do now? I suppose you want to talk about what happened that night…at the hospital…'

Max shook his head. She was too strung out at the moment to dive straight in. He needed to build a rapport with her—a professional one this time.

And for that they needed to start from scratch. The facts of the case would be discussed ad nauseam over the following weeks—he needed her to trust him. To know that he was on her side.

'No. Not right now. I want to talk about you.'

'Me?' Ali really hadn't meant it to be a squeak but she rather feared that was exactly how it came out.

Max nodded. 'You.'

Ali was confused. She'd been bracing herself to go over the whole horrible mess again. Had just about made herself sick over it. 'I don't understand…'

'I know about the case, Ali. I know it inside out and back to front. And, trust me, we're going to go over and over it again with a fine-tooth comb. For now, I want to know what a file won't tell me. I want to know your favourite colour and what books you read and whether you've travelled and if you've had chicken pox. To understand you, to understand how this predicament evolved, to help you, I need to know who you are. I need a sense of you.'

Ali sobered. This she hadn't expected. But he was so sincere, his gaze gentle and full of empathy.

And she trusted him.

'My favourite colour is yellow. Not a soft gentle yellow you'd find in a nursery but bold, like sunflowers. I don't get time to read unless you count journals but the times I do I like to read something with a happy ending. I've travelled a lot both here and overseas. Tuscany is my favourite place. Yes, I've had chicken pox. I was sixteen and it knocked me flat. I did nothing but sleep for a week and avoid looking in the mirror. It was hideous.'

She dropped her gaze briefly, embarrassed by the rush of words. She raised her eyes and blasted him with a direct stare. 'What else?'

Max blinked, a little taken a back for a moment, then laughed. 'Okay then. We're obviously going to need to work on your technique for court.'

It was Ali's turn to blink. 'My technique?'

He nodded. 'You only answer the question. There's no need to elaborate. The more information you give, the greater potential for trouble. You should have just said, yellow, fiction, yes and yes.'

Ali felt as if she'd just flunked court preparation 101. She stared glumly into her drink. 'Oh.'

'It's okay,' Max assured. 'I'll go through all this with you.'

Ali glanced at him. There was so much for her to learn before she even got to court. 'So you would have answered those questions how?'

'Orange, biographies, yes and no.'

The startling efficiency of his quick-fire response was mildly depressing. Would she ever be that cool, calm and collected under cross-examination?

'And the long answers are?'

Max smiled. 'Orange, that blood orange you see at sunset as all the colours start to bleed into each other. I too don't have a lot of time to read anything other than work-related things, but I love biographies because other people's choices fascinate me. I've travelled extensively and I also love Tuscany, although I have a soft spot for Prague. And, no, never had chicken pox.'

Ali much preferred his long answers. She was far more comfortable with Max the man, than Max the lawyer.

Even if he had seen her naked.

'I hope you've had the vaccination. Chicken pox can be pretty brutal as an adult. I had a patient my first year out, a fit twenty-three-year-old, muscle-bound footy player, who wound up in Intensive Care with it. Went to his lungs. He arrested twice.'

Max chuckled. 'I'm betting you have a medical anecdote for every occasion, right?'

Ali chewed on her bottom lip. She did have a habit of being a walking, talking heath alert. Something that had always annoyed her ex.

She shrugged. 'Sorry. Occupational hazard.'

Max shook his head. 'Not at all. It's good to know. I'll arrange to get the shot as soon as possible.'

Ali felt awkward beneath his calm grey gaze. After going to bed with him on a mere hour's acquaintance, then crying and throwing up in front of him today and now this, he probably thought she was a nutcase. And she suddenly couldn't bear the thought of it.

'You shouldn't take your health for granted.'

Ali cringed. God, she sounded waspish. *Shut up. Just shut up.*

Max nodded. 'I agree.'

Their meals chose that moment to arrive and Ali could have kissed the waiter. The aroma of perfectly charred beef hit her empty stomach and it growled.

'This smells divine.' Her mouth watered as she picked up her knife and fork.

Max drifted the conversation to film and television as they ate. Ali was more relaxed now, which was exactly where he wanted her for the more difficult questions to follow. Listening to her speak, her low husky laugh, took him back to Friday night, and for the duration of the main meal he conveniently forgot that it could never happen again.

'Okay, I'm stuffed full,' Ali said, pushing her empty plate away and slouching back against her chair. She rubbed her hand over her belly.

Max watched the action. She'd removed her jacket and the burgundy silk of her blouse slid over the skin beneath with seductive ease. Her hand stopped abruptly and he dragged his gaze upwards. Ali was watching him, her olive eyes darkening.

For a moment neither of them breathed.

'Would you like the dessert menu, sir?'

This time it was Max's turn to be grateful for the arrival of the waiter who, oblivious to the sudden electrification of the air currents, was efficiently clearing the table.

'Ah…' Max needed a second or two to get his thoughts back in order. 'Ali?'

Ali, her breath short in her chest, gratefully looked at the waiter and shook her head. 'I couldn't possibly fit another thing in.'

'Not even some double-chocolate-coated cherries?' the waiter enquired. 'They're a house speciality and absolutely delicious.'

'Oh, yes, I can vouch for that,' Max agreed, his head finally back in the game. 'In fact bring us a bowl—I'll eat them if she doesn't. And some coffee?' He raised an eyebrow at Ali.

She nodded. 'Flat white would be good.'

'Same for me,' Max said. The waiter nodded and left with the plates.

Max glanced back at Ali. That errant curl had flopped in her eye and he almost reached out to pluck it away.

Almost.

But that would be crossing any number of professional boundaries. And he'd already crossed one too many.

'So…' He ignored the curl. 'Why did you become a doctor?'

Ali's heart, still recovering from their incendiary stare of a few moments ago, thrummed nineteen to the dozen. She sucked in a breath and reached for something light to dampen the crackling atmosphere. She just hoped her voice didn't shake as much as her hands.

'Well, that's a long story.' She cocked an eyebrow. 'Do you want the court version or can I elaborate?'

He knew she didn't mean it to sound flirty but he felt the husky timbre of her voice deep inside his groin. He gave her a grudging smile. 'I've cleared my schedule.'

Ali nodded slowly. At least this was safer ground than where they'd just been.

'I didn't always want to be a doctor. Not like most of my colleagues. Growing up, I wanted to be anything from the prime minister to a fairy.'

Max chuckled. 'I would have liked to have seen that.'

Ali watched as Max's dimples came out to play and found herself grinning in response. 'Unfortunately there were no universities for fairies.'

'Very short-sighted,' Max murmured, absently rubbing at his jaw.

Ali smiled and nodded as the rasp of his stubble stirred memories from Friday night, almost obliterating the reason she'd become a doctor. But it encroached like a big black cloud anyway, wiping the smile from her face. She dropped her gaze to the table where she traced a pattern with her finger on the tablecloth.

'I had a cousin—her name was Zoe. We were the same age and incredibly close.'

A flash of Zoe's strawberry-blonde hair wafted elusively through her mind, bringing a sharp stab of unexpected grief. But grief was like that—just when you thought you'd cried the last tear another whammy hit you from out of the blue.

'We were both only children and she lived three doors down and, well…we were inseparable.'

Max watched her doodle patterns and waited silently for her to continue, a sharp sense of foreboding refusing to lift its heavy hands off his shoulders.

'She was diagnosed with a brain tumour when she was sixteen. She wanted to be a neurosurgeon from the moment they first saw that ugly white blob on her CT scan. She had a plan to rid the world of brain tumours.'

Max scanned the top of her downcast head. 'What happened?'

Ali looked up from the table cloth. 'The cancer killed her. She didn't even last a year.'

It had been a terrible time in their family.

Dark. Long. Bewildering.

'At the end…the day before she died…I promised her I'd take the baton from her and never let it go.'

Max saw the shadows in her gaze intensify. Was Zoe's fervour living on in Ali or had Ali been living a lie? Trying her best to keep a deathbed promise to someone she'd loved?

Had it been a cross too big to bear?

'Do you ever wonder what you would have

been if Zoe was still alive? Do you regret making such a big life decision at sixteen?'

Ali shook her head without hesitation, her eyes glittered with purpose. 'No. Never. I love my job. And I'm a damn good surgeon, too. I can't imagine doing anything else...'

Except she had to—now. It didn't matter how good she was, she doubted she could ever go back after the trauma of the last year.

After the court case.

'Although, I gotta say coffee-shop girl is pretty damn cushy. Compared to being a surgeon it's a picnic.' She favoured him with a weak smile. 'It's a hell of a lot less stressful.'

Max heard the rawness behind the words and wasn't fooled by the feeble smile. What Ali was going through emotionally was very familiar to him. Most of his medico-legal clients wanted to chuck it all in by the time they got to him.

'You'll feel differently. Eventually. I promise.'

Ali shook her head. 'No,' she said emphatically. 'There are two things I'm never doing again. Going back into medicine and falling for another man.'

Max regarded her serious face. He would have tried to dissuade her again except he understood how she felt about being emotionally vulnerable to another human being again. That he could definitely relate to.

'I always tell my clients to never make any decisions until after it's all over. And besides,' he said, lightening his tone to a tease, 'what else could you do? There are still no fairy universities.'

Ali managed a faint quirk to her lips. 'Who says I have to do anything, right? I could be a lady of leisure travelling all over the world. Or become a llama farmer. Or write a book.'

Max wasn't fooled for a moment. There was no excitement in Ali's voice for any of her suggestions. No passion. Her tone was flat; her eyes lacked the sparkle he'd seen when she'd told him about Zoe.

'You did all you could, Ali. Nathaniel Cullen's death was not your fault.'

Ali flinched as she heard the name again. Just when she'd thought she was immune to it, it jabbed right into her soft, spongy, bruised middle.

'Well, you have to believe me, you're my lawyer.'

Max shook his head. 'An internal hospital review believed it. An independent review commissioned by us believed it. The coroner believed it. I've been through each and every one. You, the hospital, have no case to answer.'

Ali bit down hard on her lip. She would not cry in front of this man again. 'And yet here we are, being sued anyway.'

'I've been doing this a long time, Aleisha, and I've defended my fair share of guilty clients and, believe me, you are not one of them.' He shifted in his chair. 'His parents are grieving. They're angry. They want to blame somebody. And they want their day in court. They want to be able to tell their story to a judge.'

Ali nodded. 'I know.'

And she did know. Heck, she even understood their motivations. She remembered how she'd felt when she'd lost the baby. She'd wanted to blame someone.

Anyone.

She'd wanted a focus for the maelstrom of feelings. A distraction from the overwhelming distress of being pregnant one day, growing a tiny human being, and then suddenly…not.

She'd chosen Tom. But it hadn't helped.

'But we're going to win this,' Max murmured. 'I promise you.'

Ali gazed into the steady grey depths of his eyes, desperate to believe him. She didn't even register the waiter placing her coffee down or slipping a little white bowl of cherries between them.

After a moment she said, 'I'm going to hold you to that. We fairies-in-waiting take our promises seriously.'

Max's chuckle made her shiver all over and

his smile oozed confidence as he popped a chocolate-covered cherry in his mouth and offered her the bowl.

CHAPTER SIX

A FEW days later Ali was sitting around the law firm's oval boardroom table surrounded by men in suits murmuring to each other as they waited for Max to make an appearance.

She wasn't sure if it was because she was the only female amidst seven men but the room seemed oppressively masculine. From the dark wood panelling to the polished mahogany table to the heavy brocade drapes obscuring the sunshine and river view, it was as testosterone charged as a football locker room.

Ali smiled to herself at the image of a jock-strap carelessly flung and snagged on the corner of the gilt-framed, dark-as-night oil painting hanging on the opposite wall.

It was that or scream.

'You okay, my dear?'

Ali turned to the man beside her who had already asked her the same thing twice. Dr Reginald Aimes, the hospital's CEO, had been a tower of strength during this last year and his grandfatherly concern had been most welcome.

But his fussing today was getting on her last nerve.

'I'm fine, Reg,' she said a little more testily than she should have. 'I just want it to be over.'

'As do we all, Aleisha.' He patted her hand. 'As do we all.'

The door opened abruptly and Ali flinched as her pulse skyrocketed. She was pretty sure it was the accumulated tension. Her nerves were shot these days. A year ago she'd had cast-iron control of everything. All had been well and her surgeon's hands had been steady and sure.

Nowadays the earth always felt unsteady beneath her.

But she couldn't discount Max's enigmatic presence either. He strode into the room with a purpose that bordered on arrogant, ushering in a potent mix of sex and charisma.

It was as if, for a moment, all the oxygen had been sucked from her lungs and she were back in his bed, underneath him, letting him obliterate the stench of a harrowing year.

Had it been almost a week? It felt like an hour ago.

All the other suits faded to grey as he dominated the room.

'Good afternoon, gentleman,' Max said. He nodded at Ali. 'Aleisha.' Then he sat.

'Ali,' she corrected.

Reg calling her Aleisha was just his old-fashioned sense of propriety and she'd long ago given up correcting him, but Max…

Max said Aleisha in a way that put so much distance between them she almost winced. And the last thing she needed right now was a distant lawyer. As unfortunate as sleeping with him had turned out to be, she'd felt that it at least connected them.

As if he now had a personal stake in this case.

That somehow he'd go that extra yard.

Max, ignoring the shine of her mouth and the way her soft pink blouse outlined her breasts, dismissed the correction with a flick of his wrist. 'I think it's best to stick with Aleisha or Dr Gregory.'

Ali was the woman he'd slept with.

Aleisha was a part of his case and his client's star witness.

And God knew, as she continued to look at him with those big olive eyes that were taking him right back to Friday night, he needed every professional boundary he owned firmly in place.

The door opened again and a matronly, middle-aged woman entered. She took a seat next to Max where a stenography machine had been positioned on the table.

'Everyone, this is Helen. She'll be taking notes.'

As naturally as she was breathing, Ali's astute medical gaze took in Helen's enlarged knuckles as she placed her fingers on the keys and she absently wondered if the stenographer had seen a doctor about the arthritis.

There was a general murmur of welcome and Max immediately felt more businesslike with Helen beside him. Now all he had to do was ignore the fact that he'd dreamt about eating chocolate-covered cherries off Ali's body for the past three nights.

'Welcome, everybody. Thank you for taking time out of your busy schedules so we could all meet as one. I will of course be talking to you all individually over the next few days as I do my final preparations for the court case that's scheduled week after next, but it's important to have at least one meeting with everyone present.'

There were more general murmurs of agreement around the table.

'For now though we're going to start with Dr Gregory's testimony and then we'll follow the chronology of the incident and talk to each of you in turn as the events unfolded.'

Max shuffled some papers in front of him then glanced up at his captive audience. 'Any objections?'

Ali swallowed. God, he already sounded like a lawyer. His voice even seemed different. It was still low and smooth but there was a briskness about it that ruined the languorous melody she'd instantly noticed at the bar the other night.

Max braced himself, fixing a calm neutral smile to his face as he looked at Ali. 'Dr Gregory, why don't you go through what happened the night Nathaniel Cullen died?'

Ali searched his unwavering gaze for a sign of the man she'd slept with after knowing him for a mere hour. For the man who'd tempted her with chocolate-covered cherries.

But he wasn't there.

A cool professional had taken his place.

Her heart thudded painfully in her chest. She'd told this story a hundred times. Practically everyone in the room had heard it that many times too.

It should be getting easier.

But it wasn't.

She took an unsteady breath. 'Okay.'

Max heard the quiver in her voice and was surprised by the urge to reach across the table and give her hand a squeeze. Instead he settled for an encouraging nod and a low, 'No one is judging you here, Aleisha.'

Ali bit back the natural habit of correcting the use of her name. She could see some warmth creep back into his gaze and for that he could call her whatever he damn well pleased.

'It was bedlam that night…' Her voice didn't even sound as if it belonged to her as a familiar rush of emotion bloomed in her chest and threatened to close off her throat. Reg patted her hand again and she took a sip of water.

She hated appearing weak in front of these suited men—her superiors. Surgeons had to be tough, detached, uncompromising.

It was an art she'd never quite perfected.

She knew it made her a better surgeon, a better doctor, just as she knew some of these men thought it made her unsuitable for the rigours of the job.

No doubt Max also thought it made her a terrible witness.

And that was unacceptable.

Ali cleared her throat and looked Max directly in the eye. 'I had a fifty-seven-year-old male patient with an evolving neurological deficit at the same time Nathaniel arrived in the emergency department accompanied by his mother.'

'That was at—' Max consulted his notes 'two in the morning?'

Ali nodded. 'Yes.' She took another sip of water. 'He'd presented almost twenty-four hours post falling out of bed complaining of a headache. He was stable neurologically and both he and the aneurysm patient were scanned one after the other.'

'Nathaniel first?'

'Yes. I reviewed Nathaniel's results as Mr Todd was being scanned. They revealed a very small extra-dural haematoma, two mm wide with no midline shift. Given Nathaniel's excellent neurological condition I decided to manage him conservatively as per protocol by closely monitoring him in our HDU and repeating the CT scan the next day.'

'This is standard practice?'

'Yes.'

Max made a notation, then nodded at her to continue. He could see how weary she was of the story but he wanted to hear it in her own words from her own mouth.

'What next?'

'Mr Todd's CT revealed a large leaking cerebral aneurysm requiring emergency surgical intervention. We were knife to skin within half an hour.'

Max nodded as he consulted his notes again. 'Nathaniel deteriorated while you were operating on Mr Todd?'

'Yes,' Ali confirmed. 'I was phoned in Theatre approx three hours later by my surgical resident. Nathaniel had just had a grand mal seizure and blown a pupil. He was drowsy but it was hard to assess whether this was post-ictal or due to the evolving extra-dural.'

He frowned. 'That's not typical, right?' He consulted his notes. 'Such a late deterioration?'

Ali shrugged. 'There was nothing typical about this case. But it's certainly not unheard of. Typically if someone was going to have an acute deterioration it would usually happen within a few hours post the original injury. Extra-durals are arterial bleeds so they can rapidly accumulate and the patient can just as rapidly decompensate as happened with Nathaniel.'

'Okay' He nodded. 'What then?'

'I told Jonathon, the resident, to get him to Theatre stat. I was just about finished with the clipping procedure and I had a senior resident with me who was perfectly capable of closing. I left Theatre Four and went straight into Theatre Eight where I scrubbed up again as they got Nathaniel on the table.'

'How long until you got knife to skin this time?'

'From the phone call? About fifteen minutes. But there was so much blood...'

Ali dropped her gaze to her water glass. Even now she could see its bright rich colour spilling over the green drapes, flowing to the floor, pooling around her clogs.

She'd heard about such cases, hell, she'd

been no stranger to massive loss of blood on more than one occasion in the ER, but she'd never expected to witness it coming from an eighteen-year-old's head.

She'd never forget the blood.

She returned her gaze to him. 'I couldn't stop the bleeding. He arrested on the table and we couldn't revive him.'

She willed herself not to beseech him. She hadn't done anything wrong. She hadn't been negligent. Nathaniel Cullen had sadly been just another horrifying statistic. Another patient that despite medical advances and a hospital full of whizz-bang technology they just hadn't been able to save.

Simply put—he'd been unlucky.

But she wanted Max to understand that there was nothing she could have done. That her treatment had been no different from that any other doctor would have given that night including her consultant, Neil Perry, who sat opposite her.

Tom had asked her continually what she'd done wrong, where she had erred. He hadn't understood that sometimes, no matter what you did, patients died.

Did Max?

Max gave her a moment or two. Her bald statement had been flat and emotionless but there was pain in the depth of her eyes glowing like a freshly minted coin.

He was used to this level of emotion. He dealt with people and situations that were highly charged and rarely black and white. And he'd always been able to separate himself from the emotion.

But Ali's pain reached deep inside his bones.

The need to vindicate her overwhelmed him.

'What happened next?' he asked while he battled with his keen legal mind for a modicum of professionalism. 'You told the parents?'

Ali nodded. 'Yes. By this stage both Deidre and Gordon were at the hospital.'

'And how did that go?'

Ali blinked. 'How do you think it went? I had to tell them their son was dead. It was awful.'

Max nodded, letting her derision wash past him. He'd done some pretty damn difficult things in his job but he couldn't even begin to imagine the enormity of having to tell someone their loved one had passed away.

How many times had she done that?

'Were they angry at you, at the hospital, at that stage? Did they threaten to sue that night?'

Ali shook her head. 'No, at that stage they were too…broken. They were blaming themselves, saying they should have brought him in the previous night.'

Interesting. Max scribbled a quick note. 'Would that have made a difference?'

'Most likely not. As I said earlier the size of his extra-dural on admission almost twenty-four hours post injury was only two mm. I suspect there may have been nothing to find for many hours. Had he presented immediately I would have treated him the same—CT scan and close observation.'

'Okay, good, thank you,' he said. He held her gaze as he smiled at her. 'I know it's something you've been over and over ad nauseam. I appreciate your patience, Aleisha.'

Ali's gaze tangled with his as his gentle words soothed the raw wound that he'd just prodded again. It was almost as if he'd whispered into her ear. Even the way he said her full name laid gentle fingers against her skin.

The room shrank; gooseflesh broke out on her arms.

Breaking eye contact, she reached for her glass. 'No worries,' she murmured.

Max, realising he was staring at the curve of her neck and remembering how'd she'd arched her back when he'd kissed her there, also dropped his gaze.

A tsunami of lust fogged his vision and he shuffled the papers in front of him, hoping it looked purposeful instead of erratic.

Was he going to want her every day of the coming weeks?

Maybe he should have followed Pete's advice after Tori had left and put himself out there.

Got it out of his system.

He was obviously suffering from an over-dose of testosterone now he'd broken his very long dry run. He'd forgotten how great sex was and now he was going to have to sit next to the very woman who'd reminded him, day after day, and not be able to do a damn thing about it.

He looked up to find the entire table, includ-ing Helen, looking at him expectantly.

Get a grip, man!

'Dr Perry, I believe you were the next one in-volved chronologically, followed by Dr Aimes and then the police.'

Ali was grateful that the following three hours required very little input from her other than the odd clarification or two, even if it was disconcerting to realise that Max had barely looked at her since he'd had to during her testi-mony.

In fact he seemed to be avoiding it. Even when he'd sought to clarify a point with her.

Was that a good thing or a bad thing?

She spent every minute of the three hours wondering.

By the time the meeting broke up she was

tired and tense just about everywhere, a headache forming. Max disappeared out of the door with Reg and the other suits leaving only her and Helen in the room. She was suddenly strangely reluctant to leave this oppressively masculine space. In here people seemed to know what they were doing—things were certain.

Out there, nothing seemed sure.

Ali was distracted from her thoughts as Helen, whose fingers had tapped away for hours, rubbed absently at her disfigured knuckles as she packed up.

'How long has your arthritis been this bad?' Ali asked.

Helen looked up, surprised. 'Years…I just live with it now.'

'Stenography can't help,' Ali observed.

Helen shrugged. 'It's my job.'

'Are you under a specialist?'

Helen shook her head. 'Just my GP.'

Ali tutted at the older woman. 'Here,' she said, fishing around in her handbag for her purse. She located it and extracted the business card she was after. She stood and passed it to Helen as Max re-entered the room. 'He's a good guy. Tell him I referred you.'

'Trying to steal the best stenographer in the business?' Max joked.

Helen laughed and took the card. 'Thanks, Dr Gregory.'

Ali sat again as Max, who had relieved the arthritic stenographer of her load, departed the room with Helen. Her headache tightened its steely band across her forehead a little more and she propped her elbows on the table and cradled her face in her palms.

Listening to her professional life being discussed, her every action, every word being dissected, had been harrowing and Ali rubbed at her temples trying not to think about it.

'You should go home, put your feet up and relax.'

Ali didn't have to look up to know who it was but the deep husk in his voice ensnared her in its sticky trap, drawing her gaze in his direction regardless. He lounged in the doorway, one shoulder propped against the jamb, his jacket finally removed, his shirt cuffs turned up to his elbows, his hands stuffed deep into his pockets.

'Headache?'

Ali nodded. 'Harrowing session.'

He looked at his watch and pushed off the jamb. 'It's after six. Come with me—I've got some pills in my office.'

After six? It had been hard to tell the passage of time with the curtains closed. 'Isn't pill pushing illegal?' she said, forcing a light teasing note into her voice.

It had been so serious the last three hours, if she didn't get some relief from it she was going to crack up.

Max lazed back against the jamb again and gave a half-smile. 'I don't think paracetamol counts. And anyway, I'm giving them to you, not selling them.'

'Ah, but that's how you get me hooked. Give me a free taste and *bam*, suddenly I can't go without.'

Max felt the breath seize in his lungs. That was exactly what had happened to him. She'd given him a taste of her and now he couldn't think of anything else. He'd been thinking about those damn curls brushing his chest all afternoon. He'd barely taken anything in.

Thank God for Helen and her notes.

Ali watched as Max stilled and his grey eyes darkened to slate. She suddenly realised her words spoken in jest could be misconstrued and Max had most definitely misconstrued.

She too stilled as their gazes locked. Where the hell did she go from here?

Max recovered first. 'Well, I know a good lawyer if your habit ever gets you into trouble.'

God help her, she knew a good lawyer too. And he was leading her right into trouble.

He was trouble with a capital T.

It was another moment or two before Ali broke eye contact and rose from the chair.

'Thank you, some paracetamol would be much appreciated. I normally carry some with me but I appear to be out.'

Max breathed again as she made her way around the table. But it was only momentary. As she walked towards him he got his first glimpse of her fully clad body.

A skirt. She was wearing a skirt.

And not like the one she'd worn to the bar the other night, that was loose and floaty, that skimmed and hinted. No, this was one of those straight business skirts that moulded and clung and barely reached her knees.

Perhaps if he didn't already know in shocking intimate detail what was under that skirt, it wouldn't have mattered so much. But he did— and now he was reminded of every inch.

Seriously? How was he supposed to think of her as Dr Aleisha Gregory, witness, when she was wearing that skirt?

The kind of skirt that was made to be slid up stockinged thighs...as she straddled him...in his car seat.

Ali felt her cheeks warm as Max's gaze lingered on her hips and legs. When he finally dragged his eyes back up to her face they'd darkened to graphite.

Their gazes locked for a moment. The heat from his sizzled along her nerve endings and Ali had the insane urge to pose for him. Rock one hip to the side, plant a hand on her waist, thrust her chest a little.

Max gave himself a stern mental shake and pushed off the doorjamb. 'Follow me.'

The gentleman in him should have gestured her to precede him but no way was he going to expose himself to every swing of her delectable hips outlined in a swathe of black cling wrap. It had been a long day and that skirt should come with a highly flammable warning.

Ali's legs were decidedly wobbly as she followed his long stride through the corridors to his office. Her heart beat a little too fast, her breath came a little too quick. And the hard points of her nipples rubbed painfully against the fabric of her bra with each step.

It was torture here in his jet stream as Max's sex-in-a-bottle cologne mixed with his arrogant masculinity. By the time she stepped into his office she was a nervous wreck.

Max, grateful for activity, sat in his chair and searched through a couple of drawers before he located his stash of paracetamol. He looked up.

Big mistake.

She was standing directly in front of his desk, her skirt at eye level. And he suddenly realised she could straddle him just as easily in this chair as she could in his car.

No, no, no.

Annoyed at himself for the images he didn't

seem to be able to erase, he thrust the blister pack at her. 'Bottled water over there.' He jerked his thumb over his shoulder to indicate the bar fridge behind him.

Ali blinked at his harsh tone but took the offering without comment. By the time she'd retrieved a bottle of water, swallowed two tablets and turned back to face him, he was standing at the door looking cranky and impatient.

He was holding his briefcase in one hand and his jacket in the other. 'Ready to go?'

Ali could feel her ire rise. 'You don't have to wait for me. I'm perfectly capable of finding my own way out of the building.'

'Don't be ridiculous,' he dismissed. 'I'm leaving, you're leaving. I'll see you out.'

He was pretty sure he could be trusted not to jump her in the lift.

Ali didn't know what had come over him but she didn't like this Max at all. She hoped it was courtroom Max because he sure as hell was surly.

'Fine.' She strode to the doorway, her chin up, and sailed right past him.

Too late Max realised as he fell in behind her he was about to get a close-up view of her backside whether he liked it or not. He gritted his teeth and deliberately fixed his gaze on a point in the centre of her back.

But then the bounce of her curls drew his

gaze and he remembered anew how they had felt trailing over his skin as she had gone down on him.

They stepped into the lift in silence, each taking an opposite wall. Max pushed the G button and stared studiously at the floor. Silence grew large between them until Ali couldn't stand it any more.

'What do you think of a travel agent? They look like they lead a very glamorous life.'

Max frowned and lifted his gaze. 'What?'

'As a career choice, after the court case?'

'Well, I'm not sure how you're going to fit that in around being a neurosurgeon.'

'I told you, I'm not going to do that any more.'

He rejected the suggestion with one arrogant shrug. 'Of course you are.' Then he returned his gaze to the floor.

Ali bit back a retort and reached for calm. 'Is everything okay?' she asked. 'Did I not do good today?'

Max almost groaned out loud. 'You were fine,' he dismissed testily, glaring at her.

Ali blinked. 'You seem mad at me.'

He sighed. 'I'm not mad at you, Aleisha.'

He was mad at himself.

Ali glared back at him as calm deserted her and the throb in her head intensified. She hated being called Aleisha and she'd just had three solid hours of it.

'For God's sake,' she snapped. 'We're not in the boardroom now—can you please just call me Ali?'

Max felt the waves of hostility rolling off her clash and duel with his. He jabbed his finger at the red stop button and the cab ground to a halt.

Ali gasped as she clutched the rail behind her. 'Are you crazy? What the hell are you doing?' she snapped.

Max switched his jacket to his other side and buried his free hand deep into his pocket lest he lunged for her. Which was exactly what he wanted to do. Grab her, lift her against the wall, slide his hands beneath that damn skirt and do her right here, right now.

'I can't call you Ali. Not now.' He glowered. 'Ali's the woman I've seen naked. I kissed her toes and licked her all over. For God's sake, Aleisha, I was buried inside you most of last Friday night.'

He removed his hand from his pocket to rake it through his hair. 'Ali's the name I called out as I came.'

Ali watched the agitated rise and fall of his chest and knew hers had followed suit. She could hear her breath roughen at the images he evoked.

She could almost feel the heat of his whisper as he'd groaned *Ali* in her ear.

Her arms broke out in goose bumps.

He stuffed his hand back into his pocket. 'I need to call you Aleisha. And I need to start right now. Ali is a woman I had one of the best nights of my life with. Aleisha is a witness. My client's witness. If I slip in court, call you Ali, they'll know. The judge, the opposing team, *your* hospital board—they'll all know. Because it'll be in my voice.'

Ali was stunned by his diatribe. He hadn't moved any closer, he was sticking firmly to his side, but she felt skewered to the spot by the barely leashed desire she saw burning in his graphite eyes.

Deep inside, her muscles contracted.

Max watched her watch him. He was mesmerised by the way the buttons of her blouse strained as she sucked air in and out of her lungs. He pushed his butt against the lift wall a little harder.

'Look, the truth is I'm very attracted to you and I haven't been attracted to anyone for a long time. God knows that damn skirt's driving me nuts and I'd like nothing more than to pin you against that wall—' he jabbed his finger in the direction of the wall she was leaning against '—and have my way with you. And if it wasn't for this...'

Ali swallowed, her throat suddenly dryer than a fallen autumn leaf, her pulse roaring through her ears. She looked at him for a moment or two seeing the possibilities, the fun they could be having, if the court case weren't between them.

'Yeh.' She nodded. 'If it wasn't for this…'

Max regarded her for a moment. 'So please, for the love of God, can we just stick with Aleisha?'

'Okay…Godfrey.'

There was silence for a moment, then Ali watched as his frown slowly slipped, his dimples flashed and he laughed. It slid between them as it had on Friday night and dissipated the tension to a low sizzle. She found herself laughing too.

'Touché,' he murmured.

Then he punched the ground button again and the lift lurched back into working order. The doors were opening at their destination ten seconds later.

'Go home,' he said, striding out of the lift. 'Get a good night's sleep.' *One of them might as well.* 'Tomorrow is a full day of prep.'

Ali followed him at a slower pace. Home wasn't that appealing. Kat was on a date with Pete and she didn't feel like being alone. 'I don't suppose you fancy getting a drink. Maybe a bite to eat?'

Max stopped abruptly and turned. His eyes raked her up and down. 'In that skirt? I don't think so.'

Ali blushed. 'I didn't mean…it wasn't… I'm not coming on to you.' Surely they could temper their attraction for each other in a restaurant full of people?

Max gritted his teeth as her 'coming on to you' had a predictable effect in his underpants. The still-open lift doors beckoned.

'I just thought maybe we could talk about the case away from the formality of your office,' she clarified. 'Like we did at Cha's.'

'I know. But I don't trust myself around that skirt. Here,' he said, reaching for his wallet and pulling out a business card. 'This is my mobile and home phone numbers. If you want to talk outside the office, I think we'd better stick to the telephone.'

She took the card from him and noted how studiously he avoided touching her. He looked so serious it was hard to imagine, despite the pulse of sexual awareness prickling between them, that they'd ever been intimate.

'Anything I need to know in particular for tomorrow?'

'Yes,' he grouched. 'For God's sake, don't wear that skirt. Ever again.'

And he turned on his heel and strode away.

CHAPTER SEVEN

As she had feared the apartment was lonely when she opened the door brushing raindrops off her hair.

Kat had marched in with her bags a month after Tom had moved out and completely taken over. Ali had protested at the time, had wanted to be left alone to lick her wounds, but now she couldn't imagine her two-bedroom flat without Kat filling it with chatter and laughter. Making it feel like a home.

Ali flicked on the television so the house didn't seem so silent. She poured herself a glass of wine to chase away the last of her headache and then forced herself to eat some of the left-over pasta that Kat had cooked the night before and she hadn't been able to eat because she'd been too wound up.

Another advantage to having Kat around—she was an amazing cook. Ali had never eaten so well.

Then she took a quick shower, dressed in her

pyjamas, poured herself another glass of wine and slid a DVD into the player in her bedroom. She turned out the light and pulled back the covers of her bed and snuggled down to watch the action film Kat had borrowed from the video shop on the weekend.

Action films weren't necessarily her thing but there were worse ways to take her mind off things than watching Bruce Willis running around all shirtless and macho.

By the time the film finished she was half-way through her third glass of wine and feeling really mellow. Rain was beating against the roof and window pane, occasional lightning streaks illuminated the darkened room and Bruce had saved the world.

She reached for the remote to turn the television down and her gaze fell on Max's business card she'd tossed on her bedside table when she'd dumped her handbag earlier.

Before a second thought could enter her head, she was dialling his home number.

Max frowned as his phone rang at ten o'clock at night. He reached across the various files he had strewn across his bed and snatched the receiver. 'Hello?'

'So, I'm thinking movie stunt man… woman…whatever…sounds pretty wild and exciting.'

Max gripped the phone as her voice murmured into his ear just as it had the night she'd spent right here in his bed. 'Aleisha.' *He really didn't need this.* 'It's ten o'clock.'

She squinted at the clock. 'Sorry, I may be a little tipsy.' He chuckled and her nipples tightened.

'So, stunt woman, huh? What on earth brought that on?'

'Just finished watching *Die Hard*.'

'Which one?'

'Four.'

'You know Bruce would be dead a hundred times over in real life, right?'

'Of course. So?'

He smiled. 'So it's not very realistic.'

'I don't care.' The wine was making her belligerent. 'Besides, I like it when the good guy wins.'

Yeh, so did he. It was why he'd become a lawyer.

His mind drifted back to their heated exchange in the lift, which, despite the mountains of work surrounding him, he'd been reliving most of the night. 'Are you still wearing that skirt?

'No.'

Max nodded, relieved. Which lasted a beat until the possibilities of what she *was* wearing started to parade through his mind.

'Because you're wearing an old pair of

tracky bottoms and a paint-stained T-shirt that hangs like a sack on you?' he asked hopefully.

Ali looked down at her matching hot-pink vest-top and boy-leg knickers that didn't quite meet, leaving a strip of bare flesh exposed. 'Er...okay.'

Max shut his eyes tight. 'Oh, God, you're not, are you? Please tell me you're not naked.'

His voice was husky in her ear and this time everything tightened. 'Did we just move into an ethically grey area?'

'Yes. Are you?'

Ali swallowed. 'No.' Although she might as well be given how aware she was of her body right at this moment.

Max's breath huffed out in relief.

'What are you wearing?' she asked.

'Aleisha.' No way was he about to tell her he was lying on his bed in nothing but his underpants. Or that this conversation was making them decidedly tight. 'I hope you didn't ring just to talk dirty to me.'

Ali heard the warning note in his voice. 'Grey again, huh?'

'You could say.' Although *blue* may have been more accurate.

She sighed. 'Sorry.' She sipped her wine. 'But it's all your fault.'

Max chuckled at the petulance in her voice. 'You rang me.'

Before she could stop them words tumbled out. 'You've jump-started my libido,' she grumbled. 'Tom managed to kill it dead. And I was fine with that, do you hear? Fine. I was over and done with men. And relationships. And sex. But now...'

Now one night with him and sex had managed to sideline the nagging worry that constantly gnawed at the back of her brain.

That wasn't good. The worry kept her focused. She needed to stay focused.

'Now?' he prompted.

'I can't get it out of my head.'

Max heard the bewilderment in her voice but also the longing and felt his body respond. He too had thought of little else.

But he wasn't going to talk sex with her on the phone. Not with his nearly naked body hard and aching and her wearing what he suspected was also very little.

Not when he was as done with women and relationships as she was done with men.

Not when he'd drawn a line he couldn't cross.

Ali's room glowed blue-white as more lightning lit up the night sky. 'Is it raining at your place?' she asked.

Max frowned at the rapid change in subject. He glanced at his window as rain pattered and formed tiny tributaries down his pane. 'Yes.'

Ali yawned and snuggled down into the sheet a little more. 'I love a rainy night.'

The rain and her voice, low and sleepy in his ear, seemed to cocoon him in a cosy domesticity despite the fact they lived miles apart.

It was equal parts nice and terrifying.

'Was there a purpose to this phone call?'

'You don't love a rainy night?'

Max detected the slightest trace of reproach in her voice. 'Aleisha.'

Ali tried not to be disappointed at his obvious exasperation. 'No purpose…Kat's not here and…' She pushed herself up in the bed. 'I'm sorry, forgive me. Kat always says wine gives me alcohol-induced Tourette's.'

Max chuckled and felt the terrifying ebb.

'You should ask me whatever you want about the case now. I'll be scarily honest.'

'Oh,' he teased. 'You haven't been until now?'

Ali smiled, pleased to hear his tone lighten. 'Of course I have. It was just…carefully considered. Filtered. Tonight, apparently, I have no filter.'

Max smiled at her candour. A question came straight to mind; still he hesitated before he asked it. It was a question on his list but not one he'd been looking forward to asking. Maybe in her relaxed state she wouldn't freak out.

'What happened with your ex?'

Ali sucked in a breath. That was one she hadn't expected. 'Oh.' Her brain grappled with his blunt enquiry. 'Is that relevant?'

Max grimaced at the alertness to her voice. It sounded as if she'd sobered up in a second. *And he'd been enjoying sleepy Ali.*

'From what I gleaned on Friday night, the break-up occurred a year ago. About the same time as the Cullen incident. I'm thinking maybe there were extenuating circumstances we can work into the case.'

Ali felt the weight of the events that had king-hit her a year ago press her into the bed. But she wouldn't blame her personal life for her professional issues.

'There weren't.'

'Why don't you let me be the judge of that?' he murmured.

Ali shook her head. 'Tom left after Nathaniel Cullen died. Not before.'

Max dragged Aleisha's file closer. 'How soon after?'

Ali braced herself as the answer hovered on her lips. She was sick of the platitudes that little piece of info usually engendered and she most certainly didn't want to hear one from him. 'A week.'

Max's finger stilled on his pen. *A week? Jeez, he sure knew how to kick a girl when she* was down. 'Well, now, he sounds like a real charmer.'

A bubble of laughter escaped her lips at his unexpected reaction and she felt the same connection she'd felt on Friday—the camaraderie of two people who'd been through soul-destroying break-ups.

'You want to know the worst part? I'd just miscarried his baby when he told me. I was lying in a hospital bed still attached to a drip.'

Max dropped his pen and sat forward. 'What?'

'I was pregnant. Eight weeks. I'd only just found out two weeks before.'

Max didn't know what to say. The callousness of her ex's actions was shocking and the enormity of what Aleisha had been through hit him.

'So what you're saying is...you find out you're pregnant, one week later Nathaniel Cullen dies and a week after that you have a miscarriage followed closely by your fiancé ditching you.'

Ali shut her eyes tight. The cataclysmic events of a year ago didn't sound any better in his saxophone tones. 'Pretty much.'

Max eased himself back against his pillows. 'You've been through a lot,' he murmured.

She kept her eyes shut. 'It's been a bit of an *annus horribilis*,' she agreed.

'I don't suppose you've had a lot of time to grieve either.'

Ali slowly opened her eyes. 'There'll be plenty of time for that when this is all over.'

Max stared at his rain-spattered window. 'So, I take it your ex wasn't as devastated by the miscarriage as you?'

Ali snorted. 'Tom didn't want the baby from the beginning. He wanted me to get a termination.'

'The pregnancy wasn't planned?'

Ali gave a harsh laugh. 'No. The baby was a complete shock to both of us. I mean, we had talked about kids for the future, after we'd been married for a while, after I'd become a consultant.'

'So what happened?'

'We were careless, I guess. We were busy, he worked long days, often times with my shift work I worked nights—we played tag with each other's voicemail more often than not. Our sex life was sketchy but, you know, we'd been together for five years and life was crazy between his job and mine and sex just got squeezed in around everything else.'

'That happens,' Max said. God knew he and Tori had led the same frenetic existence.

'I can't take the pill because of my family history of clots and from time to time we…took educated risks. Obviously that didn't work out so well.'

Max tutted. 'Didn't you lecture me just last week on the importance of sexual health?'

'Yeh, yeh, I know. I'm a doctor, I should have known better. But you know what? It may have only been a couple of short weeks but being pregnant was the most amazing thing that ever happened to me.'

The soft note of wonder in her voice lanced his abdomen with a white-hot bolt of longing and his own thwarted desire to have a child returned with a crippling vengeance.

He drew his knees up. 'So you were pleased?'

Ali shook her head and sighed. 'It was the most inconvenient thing. The timing was wrong. We weren't married yet, I still had a good few years of exams and study, so did Tom. But…yes, I loved my baby from the second that little pink plus sign appeared. I can't remember ever wanting anything more.'

Max nodded. 'But Tom didn't feel the same way. That must have been a source of friction?'

'You could say that…I think he'd been planning on leaving for a while. He'd been seeing the other…the other woman for six months, apparently, and this obviously threw a spanner in the works. So we argued about it—a lot. The miscarriage was his get-out-of-jail-free card.'

Max noted her stumble and the huskiness in her voice when she talked about the woman who had turned her world upside down. Also the bitter edge as she described her ex's relief.

He understood too well the overwhelming sense of betrayal she felt. When he'd found out about Tori's infidelity he'd wanted to break things.

The other guy's face had been at the top of the list.

'And you were facing all this—the pregnancy and the friction with Tom—the night that Nathaniel Cullen died?'

Ali let that sink in for a moment. 'It wasn't affecting my work,' she denied.

'Of course it was,' he said as he scribbled some notes in her file.

'No.'

Max sighed. 'Just because it wasn't overt doesn't mean it wasn't affecting you. You just didn't realise it.'

'It didn't affect my judgement.'

Max ignored her. 'It could be important in the case.'

'No.' Ali sat forward. 'I don't want to have my personal life out there for the world to know. It was humiliating enough first time around.'

'How many people know?'

'Maybe a handful.'

Max hesitated for a second while he debated telling her anything more. But it was best she knew everything. 'We need to be prepared for when the other side bring it up.'

Ali flopped back against her pillow. 'What? How are they going to know?'

'They'll have had you investigated.'

She vaulted forward again. 'What?'

'That's what I'd do if I was them.'

'Isn't that…illegal?' she spluttered.

'No.'

'Well, it bloody should be,' she grouched.

Max nodded. 'It might not come up, Aleisha. But if it does…forewarned is forearmed.'

Ali rubbed her temples as the last vestiges of her headache intensified briefly. She could see he was right. 'I could be a hairdresser,' she murmured. 'I bet there aren't too many hair-dressers sued for wrongful death.'

Max chuckled. 'Probably not.'

'It'd be nice to transform someone too, don't you think? Kind of like plastic surgery. Without the permanency.'

Max's grin faded. 'You're going to be fine, Aleisha. We're going to win this case and you're going to get back on the horse.'

Ali pressed the receiver hard against her ear. Getting back on the horse was terrifying.

'No, I'm not.' It simply wasn't an option. 'Are we done with the questions now?'

Max heard the strain in her voice and wished he could be there to reassure her in person.

And to hell with the ethics.

'I think that's enough for tonight.' The rain had stopped and he capped his pen. 'Good-night, Aleisha.'

'No, wait, hold up.'

Ali didn't want to leave it on such a downer. No way was she going to be able to sleep with her problems magnified tenfold by their conversation. And spilling her guts to him had only made her more curious about his ex. The woman who'd been married to a sex god and then foolishly let him go.

Perhaps the best time to have asked was last Friday night but there hadn't been a whole lot of talking going on.

'What about you?'

Max frowned. 'Me?'

'Sure. Doesn't this work both ways? I've told you mine, it's your turn to tell me yours.'

Max laughed. *So not going to happen.* 'Ah, no.'

'Oh, come on,' Ali cajoled. 'Think of it as trust building.'

'It's not relevant to the case,' he dismissed.

'Yes, it is,' she insisted.

'How?'

Try as she might she couldn't come up with a plausible link. She sighed. 'It's relevant to me.'

'No.'

'I'm trusting you with my most personal information, Max. Don't you think a little reciprocation is warranted?'

He snorted. 'No. I don't discuss my personal life with clients.'

Ali bristled. 'We've slept together, for crying out loud. The first person you've slept with since your marriage broke down. I *am* your personal life.'

Max had to admit she made a good point. Still…

Sensing his hesitation, Ali pressed home the advantage. 'Please, the house is quiet and the second I get off this phone with you my brain's going to kick in again and I'm sick of overthinking things. Besides, we have some solidarity here.'

Max's brow scrunched into a cynical frown. 'We do?'

'Sure. My personal life's in the toilet. So is yours. It'd be really nice to hear about somebody else's woes for a change.'

Max blinked. Had she really just said that? He began to laugh. Another man might have been affronted but she was right—his personal life sucked.

At least he could still laugh.

'Thanks for pointing that out,' he said after his laughter had subsided.

'Any time.' She grinned.

There was a pause for a moment and he knew she was waiting for him to start. He brooded for a minute—where to begin?

'How long were you married for?'

Her husky question took him back to happier times when his marriage had been new and he'd felt bullet proof.

He sighed. It was as good a place as any for the whole sorry saga. 'Eight years.'

'That's a while,' she murmured.

'Yeh,' he said bitterly. 'Long enough to know someone, you'd think.'

'She wasn't who you thought she was or she changed?'

Max mentally dismissed the options. 'We wanted different things. I just didn't realise it until the end.'

Ali waited for him to say more. 'So what did you want?'

'A family. Babies.'

Ali's heart thunked in her chest. 'And she didn't?'

'Apparently not.'

Ali felt her empty aching womb contract. She understood that yearning. She hadn't before, but she did now.

Max thought back to his childhood. 'I was an only child. It was lonely.'

She understood that too. If it hadn't been for Zoe her younger years would have felt barren.

'So…' She tried to find an easy way into her question. But there wasn't really one. 'Did you guys not…talk about children before you got married?'

Max straightened his legs, displacing her file, and crossed them at the ankle. 'Of course we did.'

The question irked. He remembered all the conversations he and Tori had had about parenting and how he'd ignored the warning voice inside his gut that had known her enthusiasm for having children was not as strong as his.

It was easy to blame her. Harder to face the truth.

'Tori wanted them. As much as I did, I thought. Not as many as I did. Two, she wanted two. I was confident I could have talked her into three.'

Ali heard the nostalgia in his voice, as if he'd just remembered the ways he'd planned on talking her into another baby, and felt a stab of something deep in her chest.

Jealousy? Regret?

'But she'd just joined a new firm and wanted to establish her career and, well…we were young, there was no rush. We agreed to start talking about it in a few years, when she turned thirty.'

Ali guessed from his voice that thirty came and went and Tori had delayed but she remained silent, letting him tell it in his words.

'I mentioned it on her thirtieth birthday and she was none too pleased. Fair enough.' He shrugged. 'It was probably the wrong time to bring it up. Thirty's a milestone for a woman and I should have been focused on giving her the best day possible instead of pushing my own agenda.'

Max shook his head as he remembered that time. He'd been so one-eyed over the whole issue. He should have known then that she didn't want the same thing.

'I gave her a couple more weeks and brought it up again. She wanted more time. Six months. A year. So I waited. Six months. A year. Two years. Three years. Then the arguments started. That I was crowding her, pushing her, she needed more time.'

Ali waited for a long time for Max to continue. The silence stretched like a giant deserted highway between them. Eventually she asked, 'Did she…did she ever say she didn't want a baby?'

'No, she just kept saying, not yet, I'm not ready yet.'

And he'd bought it because he'd desperately wanted to believe that one day she would be ready.

'To be fair she was the least maternal person I knew. I don't think she ever even picked up any of her nieces and nephews. But, I don't know…I just thought that would all change when she was pregnant with our baby.'

He'd hoped anyway. He'd hoped like hell.

'That's understandable,' Ali murmured. 'I wasn't the most maternal female on the earth either but suddenly, overnight, I became this baby-obsessed nutcase.'

Max smiled. Somehow he could imagine that. Ali, her belly big with child, glowing with health and anticipation, poking her nose into every pram that passed her on the street.

He felt his abdominal muscles tighten as an image of them together, his child in her belly, wormed into his brain.

He pushed it firmly away.

'And then I came home one night and she'd gone. Her wardrobe was cleared out, her toiletries gone from the bathroom, her car missing from the garage. She left a note saying she'd met someone else and was leaving.'

Ali blinked at the neutrality of his voice. But he couldn't fool her. She knew how deep a betrayal like this cut. 'I'm so sorry, Max. That's awful.'

Max snorted at the understatement. He'd been gutted.

'We met a few days later to talk things

through. She told me she'd fallen in love with another lawyer from her firm, a new guy, she'd already moved in with him. She said she'd… never wanted a baby.'

Ali felt the sudden rawness in his voice right down to her toes. She'd seen the damage in his eyes at the bar last week but his subdued voice murmuring straight into her ear was far more potent.

'Did she say why she hadn't come clean years before?' Ali asked, her voice soft, gentle.

'Because she'd loved me and she thought she'd grow to want what I wanted. To want a baby. But she hadn't and she couldn't live a lie any more.'

The irony was not lost on Ali. She'd wanted her man to want their baby and he'd wanted his woman to want his.

In a perfect world they'd be perfect for each other.

But there was a world of ache in his voice and she wasn't convinced that he wasn't still a little in love with his ex-wife.

She waited a beat or two before asking. 'Do you still love her?'

Max gripped the phone. Tori's betrayal had cut too deep to feel anything other than contempt. Surely she knew that? Or did she still love Tom despite all that he'd done to her? He was suddenly damn sure he didn't want to know the answer to that and he was just plain weary of talking about the past.

'I think that's enough with the questions for one night, Aleisha.'

Ali shivered as his low husky tones feathered down her neck. He sounded so close he could have been in bed beside her.

Was that a yes?

'Get some sleep. I'll see you at prep tomorrow.'

The phone clicked in her ear.

CHAPTER EIGHT

Two weeks later Max was chatting to Reginald Aimes in the cavernous atrium of the courthouse the opening morning of Cullen v Brisbane Memorial when the aroma of warmed baked goods enveloped him in a cloud of intoxicating sweetness.

Despite his hearty breakfast his belly rumbled and he turned his head to identify the source just as Reg said, 'Ah, Aleisha, how are you, my dear?'

Ali, pulling close to the two men, grabbed Reg's outstretched hand and presented her cheek for his fatherly peck. 'Ready,' she said.

And she was. This thing had been hanging over her head for so long now, like a cancer. She was ready to finally be able to do something about it. To fight.

'Good.' He patted her on the shoulder. 'It'll all be over in a couple of weeks and Max is confident we'll win, aren't you, Max?'

Max dragged his gaze back from his search and smiled at her. 'Absolutely.'

She looked good. Tired, but good. He was pleased to see she'd taken his advice and dressed conservatively in dark trousers and jacket, flat shoes and minimal make-up.

Her hair was still a wild array of butterscotch curls that were utterly feminine and completely distracting but, short of asking her to cut them off, he was stuck with them.

Both in this world and the more elusive, erotic world of his dreams.

A mobile rang. Reg patted his pocket and withdrew the ringing gadget. 'Excuse me,' he said. 'I've got to take this.'

They watched Reg move away and Max indicated for her to follow him. Ali tagged after him, out of the main foyer area and along several carpeted corridors. She felt surprisingly calm as each step took them further into the bowels of the old, yet still imposing building.

She suspected it wouldn't last. No doubt the second she walked into the courtroom she'd be a blithering mess. But for now, Ali felt good.

'In here,' Max said.

Ali waited for him to unlock a door and preceded him into the room. It was nondescript and boxlike with cheap grey vertical blinds covering the only window. Six chairs surrounded a small oval table, a far cry from the monolith in Max's boardroom back at the firm, and she noted that Max's laptop and briefcase had already claimed a spot.

She turned to face him. He hadn't moved from the doorway and she quirked an eyebrow at him.

Max stood, statue-like, suspended in a cloud of sponge cake and warm croissants, unable to breathe for a moment.

It was her?

She smelled like a patisserie?

He gave an inward groan at the unfairness of it all as the overwhelming urge to nuzzle her neck surged like a symphony in his blood.

As if she weren't good enough to eat already.

Max gripped the knob hard. 'Sit.'

Ali frowned at his tense request. 'What's wrong?'

'Nothing,' he dismissed, stalking to the table and sitting down as the door clicked shut.

Ali pulled out one of the chairs and sat, aware of a small twist of tension bunching her neck muscles. 'So, should we go over the procedure for the day again?' she asked.

They'd already been over it several times, including just yesterday, but Max didn't think you could ever be too prepared.

'Good idea.' Max nodded, launching into his spiel as he tapped his pen against the desk.

Ali tried to take it all in but the set to his jaw

was making her nervous and she wondered if he knew something, some development that she hadn't been privy to.

'Is everything okay, Max?' she interrupted.

Max nodded and ploughed on, still tapping his pen. Ali was first on the witness list and he fully expected her testimony to take two days. And although he'd warned her, he didn't think she fully appreciated how gruelling it was going to be.

The last thing he needed was for her delicious scent to be screwing with his concentration. Which it was—big time! It was stirring a hunger in him that had nothing to do with his belly.

He stopped mid-sentence as another waft of her actually made his mouth water.

He threw down the pen. 'What are you wearing?'

Ali stared at him nonplussed. She looked down at her clothes. 'You said conservative. You said no skirts.'

'No, damn it,' he growled. 'I mean your perfume.'

Ali blinked. 'Vanilla oil?'

Vanilla. That was what it was. That was what was making him want to lick her neck.

'Kat gave it to me. It's supposed to be good for relaxation.'

'Is it working?'

'Yes. Or at least it was until you got all tense and cranky.'

'I'm not cranky,' he denied, but one look at her incredulous expression made him reassess. Max rubbed his forehead. 'Sorry, I…'

I, what, big boy?

I want to bury my face in your neck? I want to see if you taste the same everywhere? I want to throw you on this table and nibble you all over?

'You…don't like the perfume?'

Max stifled a groan. He rested his chin on his palm and stared at her for a moment. 'I think the problem is I like it a little too much.'

'Oh,' Ali said, her frown building and then slowly slipping as realisation dawned. 'Oh-h-h. You *like* it.'

Max gave her a grudging smile. 'I find it very…distracting.'

'Oh-h-h,' she said again, but fainter this time as his gaze strayed to her mouth and her breath seized in her chest.

They'd done well the last couple of weeks putting their first inauspicious meeting behind them. They'd both worked hard to keep things strictly business, to hack off the persistent, cloying tentacles that had attached themselves after their explosive night in bed together.

Max had even reneged on his offer for her to ring him after that first phone call had strayed into dangerous territory. He'd thought further phone contact would be unwise. That it blurred that line the case had drawn between them. And she'd agreed.

But suddenly she was back in his bed, under him and her pulse seemed to pick up the rhythm they'd set that night. She sucked in a breath as the air between them seemed to vibrate.

Max watched as her olive eyes darkened and her glossy lips parted slightly. He remembered every detail of that mouth. How it tasted, how it felt against his, where it had been.

Ali swallowed as his gaze fixed on her mouth. She vaguely heard the slow steady drum of his fingers against the table as if he was weighing up his options.

To kiss or not to kiss.

It would be easier if she knew herself which way she wanted him to jump. But she had the feeling if he pounced—ethics aside—they'd be late for court.

Very, very late.

She licked her suddenly parched lips and instantly wished she hadn't as his nostrils flared and his fingers stopped drumming. 'I could… not wear it again…'

Max pulled his hand back and tucked it safely under the desk. It was too close to temptation above it.

There was just too much temptation all round!

He considered her proposal. The case could conceivably run for two weeks—could he face that intoxicating aroma attached to her delectable skin knowing how badly he wanted to taste it, day after day, for potentially a fortnight?

Without going insane?

But if it was helping her to relax then he couldn't argue with that. It was going to be a stressful couple of weeks and if vanilla oil helped then he didn't have the right to ask her not to wear it.

'No, it's fine,' he dismissed, his tone gentler. 'I need you relaxed. Whatever it takes.'

Even if it was going to have the opposite effect on him.

The door opened abruptly then, admitting Reg and two other board members along with Max's co-counsel, Gemma Ward, and Don Walker, a representative from the hospital's insurer. Max quelled the urge to spring back from Ali. They weren't close and they hadn't been doing anything wrong.

Not really.

But he was grateful for the horde's timely arrival anyway.

Twenty minutes later Judge Veronica Davies swept into the courtroom and called the case to order. Max was pleased to have scored her. He'd been in her courtroom many times and her reputation for being tough but fair was well respected.

Max straightened his notes as the judge went through the preliminaries. Reg and Don sat on his right. Gemma sat on his left. Across the centre aisle sat Deidre and Gordon Cullen and their lawyers.

Aleisha sat on the first row of seats directly behind him but still her delicious vanilla essence reached out. It curled seductive fingers into his gut and squeezed tight. He gripped the edges of his notes harder and prayed for patience.

He concentrated instead on Aleisha's reaction to Nathaniel's mother's contemptuous look. It had devastated her and his drive to vindicate Aleisha trebled. Every day she'd come to the prep session proposing a new profession and it had become a standing joke. But Max knew that Aleisha was serious.

If things went badly in court she would never return to medicine. Hell, he was beginning to believe that she probably wouldn't even if they went well.

'Mr Sherrington?'

Max looked up from his deathlike grip on his papers. He smiled at the judge and rose. 'Yes, Your Honour.'

'Call your first witness.'

Max felt a moment's trepidation—unusual for him. He never felt anything but one hundred per cent in control in a courtroom.

But no case had ever felt this personal before.

'I'd like to call Dr Aleisha Gregory.'

And so began two punishing days of questions about that awful night. Every second was dissected—every movement examined, every decision scrutinised.

Nothing was off limits.

Not her thoughts or her notes or her state of mind or her personal life. As Max had predicted, her break-up was trotted out, her miscarriage tossed around by the opposing side. She was stripped bare before everyone until Aleisha felt like a skeleton sitting in the chair, all her flesh torn away, exposed right down to her bones.

And then after they were done taking pieces from her on the stand they spent the remainder of the week and three days into the next taking pieces from her through other people.

As if she weren't there.

I'm right here, she'd wanted to scream. *I'm sitting right here in the first row.*

The Cullens said she and the hospital were negligent.

Max argued they weren't.

And on it went. Days of hearing from endless witnesses involved in the incident that night, their view of the events put under a microscope.

An army of expert witnesses dissecting her every action, half supporting the claim of negligence, the other half refuting.

Going from home to court, from court to home utterly wrung out from doing nothing at all. Just listening to her life, her career, her hopes and dreams slowly being dismembered.

Max was her only sanity. Every morning he'd tell her she was doing well and she clung to that like a buoy in a storm-tossed ocean because the legal argument was too intense and too intimidating to believe for a moment that she might actually be winning.

And she had to win. She just had to.

'I'm thinking air hostess,' Ali said into the phone. The court case was expected to wrap up tomorrow and she knew she wasn't supposed to ring but she was feeling particularly edgy tonight.

Max, who had dozed off surrounded by paperwork, glanced at the clock. 'It's almost midnight.'

'Sorry. Can't sleep.'

Max heard the strain in her voice as several

ways to get her to sleep very unhelpfully reared their ugly, suggestive heads. 'It'll all be over tomorrow,' he murmured. 'And we're going to win.'

Ali nodded, wishing she could feel more confident. 'Right.'

'So…a trolley dolly?'

Ali shrugged. 'Why not? I could indulge my love of travel.'

'We're going to win, Aleisha.'

'And I love their uniforms.'

Max shut his eyes as a picture of Ali in a tight skirt, stockings and high heels slithered into his mind. She was leaning over him, her cleavage on display, serving him a drink and calling him *sir*. And then he was following her down the aisle, into the staff amenities, shutting the door, sliding her skirt up…

God. This was torture.

'So do I.'

Ali heard the unspoken in the low saxophone timbre of his voice. A delicious tingle spread from the hand holding the phone all the way up her arm. 'You have a thing for skirts, don't you?'

'Not usually.'

Ali gripped the phone harder as his meaning hit home. This phone call had careened quickly out of control. Maybe it was the end result of being forced to spend day after platonic day in his company when her body was craving something else entirely. When it remembered in fine detail how good they'd been together.

'Maybe you should see a doctor about that?'

'I am.'

Ali swallowed against a surge of desire thickening in her throat. 'Is he good?'

'*She* is.'

Ali's breath became choppy. 'Doesn't sound like she's cured you yet.'

Max's body tightened as the magnified sound of her rough breath brushed over his belly like a siren's call. 'Maybe I don't want to be cured?'

Ali's toes curled. 'I guess there are worse things to be hung up on.' *Even if she couldn't for the life of her think of a single one.*

Max couldn't agree more. Like vanilla and butterscotch curls and big, beautiful breasts. But this conversation was heading in the wrong direction—fast. For God's sake, there was just one night to go—he'd nearly made it. He had to pull it back.

'I think it's time we said goodnight.'

Ali stilled for a moment, a stab of disappointment mingling with relief. She should be happy he was bringing them back from the edge. *It was a completely inappropriate conversation to be having with her lawyer.*

But with her body humming like a tuning

fork it was hard to concentrate on anything else. 'Wait,' she said, dragging her body back from the edge. There had been a purpose to this phone call—sort of. 'How well do you know the judge?'

Max frowned at the phone. 'Why? Are you suggesting we bribe her?'

Ali laughed and felt some of the tension ooze from her pores. Kat, who had just come in from work, poked her head in the door and smiled at Ali. Ali waved her in and Kat flopped on the bed.

'No. It's her mole, actually.'

'Her mole?'

'Yes, the one near her top lip.'

Max rolled his eyes. He knew the one she was referring to, it was rather unmissable. 'Yes?'

'I've noticed the last few days that she's been scratching it a lot and I don't like its shape and she has such pale skin... Do you know her well enough to enquire as to whether she's seen anyone about it and perhaps suggest that she should if she hasn't? I'd do it but I'm not allowed to talk to the judge so...'

Max blinked. He'd spent the last fortnight listening to her wackier and wackier suggestions for a career change because she couldn't see what was right in front of her—she was a doctor right down to her very cute toes.

From lecturing him on getting a chicken-pox vaccination to helping Helen with her arthritis, to dishing out dermatological advice to one of the court reporters and now this. And that didn't even take into account the Band-Aid she'd produced from her handbag when a child had fallen and scraped her knee in front of them on the street the other day as they'd been walking to the car park. Or the medicated lozenge she'd dished out to Gemma, who'd come down with a hoarse throat on day three of the court case.

Whether she liked it or not—Aleisha Gregory was a born doctor.

'Says the woman who wants to be an air hostess...' he murmured.

Ali gripped the phone. Max was right—she really had to stop dishing out unsolicited medical advice. Right after the judge had her mole seen to. 'So that's a no?'

Max shook his head, resigned to his fate. 'I'll talk to her.'

Ali smiled and winked at Kat. 'Thank you.'

Max chuckled at the little note of triumph in her voice and tried not to think of her crammed into an aeroplane loo with him, her skirt around her waist. 'Say goodnight now,' he murmured, not sure he was strong enough any more to do it himself.

Ali grinned. 'Goodnight now.'

Kat watched Ali as she rang off. 'You guys seem to get along well.'

Ali fluffed the covers and avoided Kat's keen gaze. 'He's my lawyer, Kitty Kat. Nothing else.' *And it would be very foolish to think otherwise.*

'I'm just saying...'

'Don't.' Ali was pleased she'd decided to keep the one-night stand to herself. She didn't want Kat to be building castles in the air.

'We've both come out of terrible breakups and, oh, newsflash, *he's my lawyer.*' She grinned down at her friend. 'Besides...I think he's still in love with his wife.'

It was the first time she'd said it out loud and she felt instantly depressed. Just because sex with Max had been mind-blowing for her and there was obviously a strong sexual undercurrent raging between them, didn't mean he was emotionally engaged.

Kat squeezed her hand. 'Right. So best not fall for him, then.'

She nodded. 'Right.'

Ali awoke the next morning with a mass of nerves knotted in her stomach.

She thought she was going to throw up.

Even Max's 'we're going to win' assurances from their phone call last night weren't enough to untwist the knot. She hadn't really believed him then and this morning, looking at her wan reflection, big black smudges under her eyes, she still didn't.

Not even a positive prophesy from a crystal ball would have been enough to keep the doubt demons at bay.

For some Dutch courage she uncapped the bottle of Kat's vanilla oil and extracted the glistening glass dauber. She dabbed a drop or two at the base of her throat where her pulse fluttered, and dragged the warm glass behind each ear, smearing more oil there.

Sensitive to Max's predicament, she hadn't worn it after that first day. Every time he'd looked at her she'd been able to see the hunger in his eyes and, worse, had felt the answering pangs inside her intensify.

On a visceral level Ali had sensed that first day that their situation was perilously close to getting lost in the abyss of grey that made the line between black and white wavery and indistinct.

And she'd known it was best not to feed the beast.

But if there was ever a day she needed vanilla oil it was today. If she didn't relax a little she was going to blow a blood vessel or give herself glaucoma.

Today, she'd take any crutch she could get.

She inhaled as the scent surrounded her in its sweet embrace. It reminded her of baking cakes with Zoe, of porridge with brown sugar sprinkled on top, of a little bakery in Rome down beneath street level.

Happy memories. She smiled at her reflection. She was relaxing already.

Then a set of grey eyes, as grey as that abyss, flashed through her mind. She could almost feel the flare of two very male nostrils as they whispered against the skin of her throat.

Her stomach growled.

Max was engrossed in some case notes on his laptop when the aroma of vanilla undulated into the room like an exotic dancer. He turned abruptly to see Ali hesitating in the doorway.

Lust arced between them as the aroma put him right back in the middle of their flirty phone call from last night. 'Oh, God, Aleisha, really?' he groaned.

'Sorry.' She grimaced. 'I'm pretty wound up. I needed something. I figured hitting the red wine this early probably wouldn't look good to the judge.'

'It's fine,' he said even as his mouth watered.

Ali could see restraint and desire swirling like grey mist in the depths of his gaze. She could feel it rippling towards her, shimmering like fog as seductive as the devil's whisper.

She took a step back. 'I'll wait for you inside.' And she fled.

Max turned back to his laptop and sucked in a breath. Just one more day. That was all he had to get through.

Being in close contact with her for the last few weeks had been difficult with a fully charged libido—for which she was responsible. Every cell in his body was begging to touch her.

But it was all going to be over today.

Over for good.

No more weekend prep. No more squeezing her hand, clasping her shoulder, day after day, assuring her it was all going to work out.

Which was good. All good.

He'd say goodbye later today after it was done and walk away. Because he'd already got too close to this case.

Too close to her.

He'd vowed after Tori left that he was done with relationships but he was pretty sure that somehow he'd landed himself right back in the middle of one. Hell, he knew more about Aleisha Gregory after a few weeks' acquaintance than he'd ever known about his own wife.

He certainly knew she wasn't interested in a relationship.

And neither was he—the ink was practically still wet on his decree absolute.

This...thing had to end. Today.

As it happened the case didn't finish up by the end of the day. Some unexpected power outages caused a security alert and the building was evacuated twice, wasting three precious hours. Closing arguments were delivered in the dying hours of the work day and the judge decided to deliberate overnight and convene again in the morning for her decision.

Ali wasn't sure whether she wanted to cry, vomit or stamp her foot as she stood for the judge's departure. She'd psyched herself up for the big decision and it had been snatched away.

It was a major anticlimax.

And meant she had to come back tomorrow and face this all again.

Max turned to her. 'I'm sorry,' he said as her vanilla essence drove another nail into the insanity coffin.

She shook her head and sank back down into her seat. 'Not your fault.'

'It'll be quick tomorrow,' he assured. 'You don't even have to be here.'

She lifted her head and looked him in the eye. 'Yes. I do.'

Max nodded as his belly did a triple somersault with a double twist. She was one gutsy woman. Sitting in court day after day stoically listening as her life was pulled apart and not buckling under the pressure was an act of courage.

He couldn't remember admiring a woman more.

Just one more thing that scared the hell out of him.

Fifteen minutes later Ali and Max caught the lift together down to the ground floor. It was half full and they shuffled to one side, keeping a safe distance between them. The cab lurched as it began its sluggish descent and Max grabbed the rail to prevent bumping into Ali.

He was excruciatingly conscious of Ali's delicious aroma and tried not to inhale during the journey. But the lifts were as old as the building and universally acknowledged as being the slowest in Brisbane so Max doubted he'd be able to hold his breath for the duration.

Unfortunately the lift also managed to stop on every floor, admitting more and more people, pushing them closer and closer together. By the time a rowdy group of men got in on floor five they were squashed against the back wall like tinned sardines.

And Max couldn't hold his breath any longer.

His body was blocking hers from the mass

of bodies around them and his nostrils flared as they filled with her sweet macaroon scent. He felt his body respond, tighten, to their proximity and the carnal essence of her.

Her curls brushed his face and he shut his eyes as they lightly caressed his cheek with their springiness. The lift lurched to a halt at the fourth floor and their bodies bumped against each other. He reached for her hip to steady her.

Ali's stomach clenched as a heat down low mushroomed into her belly and down her thighs. She kept her gaze firmly fixed on the knot of his tie but she was hyperaware of his hand branding her, the heat of his body, the husk of his breath.

Max dropped his head slightly so his mouth was level with her ear. He shouldn't be this close—they were in a lift full of people, for crying out loud—but didn't seem to be able to stop. He nuzzled her hair for a moment then murmured, 'I want to kiss you. I know I shouldn't but I do.'

He'd been going to say that he'd talked to the judge, who had already made an appointment to see her GP, but it seemed his mouth had a mind of its own.

And the truth had a funny way of coming out.

As a lawyer, Max knew that better than anyone.

Ali, grateful for the loud buzz of conversation around her, shut her eyes as his voice whispered to every cell screaming for his touch.

'I've wanted to kiss you every day since that night.'

'Don't, Max…' she whispered, turning her head slightly towards his ear.

He groaned quietly into her neck where she smelled so, so sweet. Being with her every day and faking a professional façade while the air sizzled between them was impossible. 'I can't take much more of this.'

Ali's body swayed closer until they were touching from torso to hip. She wanted to get closer. To turn her head and mash her mouth to his, wind her arms around his neck, grind her pelvis into his.

'Tomorrow…' she whispered.

The lift bumped none-too-gently to the ground and brought Max firmly back to earth in more ways than one. But the crowd started to push forward and it was too late for Max to remember there wasn't going to be a tomorrow.

Not as she meant anyway.

Even though his body demanded it.

That when they left court tomorrow, it would be the last time they saw each other.

The triple somersault his stomach had performed earlier had scared the hell out of him.

The intensity of the way he'd wanted her just now in a crowded lift even more so.

It was better to chalk their one-night stand up to experience and move on.

Repeating it was something neither of them needed.

Max allowed himself to be propelled out of the lift, aware of Ali at his elbow. Their pace slowed as the crowd dispersed.

'So...I'll see you at nine tomorrow?' he asked.

Ali, her body still grappling with an infusion of lust that had hijacked her body, frowned at him. How could he be so together when her oestrogen receptors were shorting out?

'Ah...okay, sure...'

Her confused look made Max want to reach out and snatch her to him so he gripped his briefcase handle hard and stuffed his other hand deep in his pocket. He really had to get away from her.

And her damn vanilla essence.

He nodded. 'Bye.'

And then turned on his heel and walked away.

The phone rang at nine-thirty just as Max had finished drying himself off from his shower and he almost didn't answer it. After all he knew who it was going to be and he'd just spent two hours pounding the city pavements and the cliffs around Kangaroo Point trying to run her out of his system.

But he did anyway. Because he just didn't seem to have any self-control where Ali was concerned.

He secured the towel around his hips and snatched up the receiver on his bedside table.

'So I'm thinking lift designer.'

Max chuckled despite himself and his determination to keep the call impersonal and brief flew out of the window. He sat on the side of the bed.

'Seriously, those lifts at the courthouse are too damn slow.'

Max's smile slipped as he remembered those couple of electric minutes where he'd totally lost his mind and nuzzled her neck. He appreciated her attempt to dispel any awkwardness by making light of what happened but his body stirred beneath the towel regardless.

'Those lifts are too damn full,' he growled.

Ali, who had just speared a piece of veal tortellini, paused with it halfway to her mouth. What the hell would have happened if they'd been alone in the lift this afternoon?

'Probably just as well,' she murmured.

Max sighed as he swung his legs up on the bed and lounged against the pillows. 'Yes, I suppose you're right.'

There was a moment of silence during which the pasta stayed suspended on her fork halfway to her mouth before Ali slipped it in and forced herself to chew.

'So...' Max groped around for something to say that wouldn't get him disbarred. 'Is Kat home tonight?'

The existence of Ali's flatmate, even peripherally, was a good deterrent. God knew he was counting on Kat's omnipresent state tonight, both in the flat and his mind, to help him keep a tight rein on his libido.

'She was, of course, because we all thought today would be the day we'd know the outcome and she cooked my favourite pasta meal but her younger brother Damian, who is, shall we say, enjoying the freedoms of the city now he's at uni, rang to say he was in the lock-up for being drunk and disorderly—again—and could she come and bail him out and she was furious and told me he could just sweat it out for a few hours because I was more important but I told her not to be silly, that Damian was much too pretty to be sitting in the lock-up with pimps and drug addicts and she must go...'

Dear God, she was babbling.

'So she left reluctantly but, boy, oh, boy is she ever steamed. I think she's going to threaten to tell her parents this time if he doesn't clean up his act. She's promised not to tell the other two times but I think her goodwill has just run out...'

Max gripped the phone harder. *Great, so she was alone in the flat. Probably in her pyjamas. Lying on her bed.*

Ali cringed at the silence that followed. 'Sorry,' she apologised, poking at her pasta. 'I'm babbling...'

She speared another tortellini shell and brought it to her mouth. It dropped off before it made it to its final destination, landing on her hot-pink vest-top.

'Damn it,' she cursed, sitting up.

Max frowned. 'What?'

Ali leaned forward as she picked the food off her pyjama top, dismayed to see a huge red sauce stain on her top. 'I spilled some food on my pyjama top. Hang on,' she said, 'I'll just go and take it off.'

'Aleisha?'

There was no reply. Max stared at the receiver and then bashed it against his forehead three times as he heard rustling on the other end.

Was she trying to kill him?

Ali walked through to her en suite pulling the top over her head as she went. She threw it in the wicker hamper, then returned to the bed. She picked up the phone as she sat and pulled open her bedside drawer looking for something else to wear.

'Sorry,' she said, raising her shoulder to cradle the phone against her ear. 'Back again.'

Max shut his eyes. 'Please tell me you're not shirtless now.'

Ali's hands stilled in her drawer. The raw edge in his voice streaked straight to a place deep inside her belly. She looked down at her bare breasts. The nipples scrunched instantly. The desire that had engulfed her in the lift swamped her body again.

She was suddenly aware of the cool air on her skin. The feel of the cotton sheet at the backs of her thighs. The slight tickle as her caramel curls brushed her shoulders. The prickle of every tiny hair on her body. The hum in her blood.

She was aware, too aware, she was a woman.

She withdrew her hand from the drawer.

Would it hurt to be semi naked talking to him? She was an adult and in the privacy of her own bedroom. The idea was alluring. Enticing. Naughty...

And very, very grey.

'I'm afraid so,' she murmured huskily, swallowing against her suddenly arid throat. 'Why, what are you wearing?'

Max shut his eyes as an image of her laid out on his bed, her naked breasts bare to his gaze, formed with startling clarity. Every muscle in his body was on high alert. 'A towel.'

Ali also shut her eyes. 'So we both seem to be rather…undressed.' The thought was as alluring as it was forbidding.

Max's eyes flew open as the possibilities paraded through his mind.

Oh, no, he wasn't going there.

He couldn't.

He groped for a way to get the conversation back from careening out of control and grabbed the first ill-formed thought that came along. 'Yep, all ready for bed.' Then he realised what he'd said and hurried to clarify.

'For sleep, I meant. To sleep…'

Ali smiled. She knew what he'd meant and she grabbed hold of the conversation redirect gladly.

'I wish.' Ali doubted sleep would be easy to achieve tonight. 'I don't think I'm going to be able to sleep very much. I've barely managed two or three hours a night since the case went to court.'

Max nodded. He'd known insomnia had plagued her throughout the court case. It had plagued him since Tori had left, hence his marathon training. He'd basically run until he was exhausted.

The only time he'd slept soundly in the last

eighteen months that hadn't been fatigue induced had been the night they'd spent together.

The thoughts he'd had last night while talking to her on the phone returned. There was nothing quite like a good orgasm to induce a deep, satisfying slumber.

He shut his mind against the illicit suggestion that was forming. *Tried anyway. And failed.*

Damn it, he'd managed to shut the door on it last night, he could do it tonight.

But she hadn't been shirtless last night...

And while his mind was struggling with the door his mouth had other ideas.

'I know a good way to get you to sleep...'

CHAPTER NINE

ALI'S heart tripped in her chest at Max's low husky words. The possibilities quickened her breath.

'Is it…appropriate?'

'No.' It was very, very inappropriate. But…it wasn't as if he were sleeping with her. He was just…bending the rules a little.

Walking that fuzzy grey line.

Ali swallowed. 'What did you…have in mind?'

'Are you wearing underwear?'

Ali's heart pounded so loudly through her ears it sounded as if a brass band were playing at the end of her bed. Surely he could hear it?

'Yes.'

Max felt the soft graze of terry towelling taunt his hardness as her husky response stroked fingers of desire up the backs of his thighs and deep into his buttocks.

'Take them off.'

Ali's breath stuttered out at his shocking

suggestion. 'I don't think…I mean I'm not sure…'

Her almost maidenly hesitation inflamed his desire further. 'I want to stroke you all over. I need you naked.'

'But…' Ali groped for a modicum of sense in a brain quickly liquefying into a puddle of lust. *Was he suggesting what she thought he was?* 'You're not here.'

Max chuckled at her confusion, at her determination to hold onto sense despite the breathy quality to her voice that told him she was as titillated as he was.

'You're going to do it for me.'

Ali sucked in a breath. *Oh, God. He was! He was suggesting it.* The thought of phone sex with Max invaded and conquered every cell.

Dared she?

It was one thing to be topless and talking to him—it was naughty and he didn't have to know. It was another entirely to be naked, talking to him and…touching herself.

And him knowing.

Max could hear nothing but the tortured husky timbre of her breath. 'Take them off, Aleisha,' he murmured again.

Ali, her last skerrick of resistance obliterated by his illicit demand, whispered, 'Okay.'

She stood, holding the phone to her ear with her shoulder again as her shaking hands slipped her knickers down her thighs and past her knees. She stepped out of them and kicked them free.

Max, his own pulse loud in his ears, could just make out the rustling as Ali removed her underwear.

She'd done it. She'd actually done it.

He felt her low hoarse, 'What next?' right down to his toes.

'Lay on the bed.'

Ali, her legs suddenly as useless as boiled spaghetti, sank onto her pillow-topped mattress. The white cotton sheet felt as decadent as black satin. Her bed suddenly seemed to hover like a magic carpet.

The bedside lamp, which had always needed a brighter bulb, now bathed her body in a soft sexy light and Ali almost gasped as she watched her breasts swing and bounce seductively with every movement.

She put the phone on speaker and set it near her head. 'Okay.'

Max heard excitement and anticipation in the breathy roughness of her voice. His body ached but he ignored his own discomfort.

He shut his eyes and imagined he was lying in bed with her. 'You have the most amazing breasts,' he murmured. 'Soft but still firm. And big. I like how big your breasts are. I'm touching them, Aleisha. Can you feel it? They fill my palms. I like how my hands look on your breasts. They feel big and rough against all that softness.'

Ali felt her stomach twist deep inside at his words. Her eyes fluttered closed as his voice evoked the images he described. His hands on her breasts—caressing, stroking, kneading.

'Are you touching them? Touch them, Aleisha.'

Ali's hands seemed to move of their own volition in response to his rough command. 'Oh,' she cried out, biting down on her lip as her nipples tightened the second her fingers tentatively touched the swell of one breast.

'What?' he murmured.

Ali shivered. 'My hands are cold but my skin…my skin is hot. I have…goose bumps.'

Max almost groaned as he saw the aroused peaks of her breasts in his mind's eye. 'Your nipples are hard, yes?'

'Yes.'

'Like berries.'

'Yes.'

'Touch them,' he demanded in an urgent whisper.

Ali ran her finger lightly over a taut brown peak. She bit down on her lip as a streak of molten lust arrowed its way to her middle and oozed rivulets of sensation from her belly to her thighs.

'They feel good, don't they, Aleisha? I wish you could taste them. They taste like you, all sweetness and spice and they feel ruched against my tongue. I'm swiping my tongue across one of those hard little buds right now. I like how you do that funny noise at the back of your throat when I suck one deep inside my mouth.'

Ali heard the moan escape from her lips and drift into the air somewhere above her head. She flattened the pad of her thumb against each nipple and pushed hard to ease the tingling his words had evoked.

Max gripped the phone. 'I love making you moan. I like watching your nipple when I let it go and watch how it gets all hard as the air hits it. Put your fingers in your mouth, Aleisha, make your nipples wet for me.'

Powerless to resist the low sexy commands coming from the phone, Ali did as she was bid, smearing warm saliva on her nipples. It cooled rapidly against the heated flesh and she gasped as her nipples tightened to an almost unbearable intensity.

'You like that, don't you, Aleisha?'

Ali shifted restlessly against the bed, eyes still closed, head tossed to the side. 'Yes,' she breathed heavily as she channelled Max's hands cupping and squeezing her breasts.

Max's breath hitched at the note of sexual

abandonment in her voice. 'What else do you want, Aleisha? Tell me.'

Ali tossed her head to the side. She wanted to feel his mouth on hers, to feel him deep inside her. 'I want to...touch you...' she murmured.

Max's erection kicked hard against the confines of the towel. It would be so easy to loosen it, slip his hand down, touch himself as she was doing.

His body was all but demanding it.

But *that* he couldn't justify. In this strange new world of ethical ambiguity he seemed to be co-existing in with Ali, *that* would be taking it too, too far. That would be well and truly stepping over the line.

And this wasn't about him.

'No,' he murmured. 'This is for you. Only you.'

Ali opened her eyes, opened her mouth to protest. If he could play, why couldn't she? But then he said, 'Spread your legs, Aleisha,' and she lost her mind.

'Call me Ali,' she begged as the sheets rasped against the backs of her thighs adding to the sensual overload.

'No.' *Too, too far.*

'Please, Max,' she implored as her fingertips trailed lightly over her belly.

He ignored her. 'Are you ready for me down

there? I can still remember how you taste. I dream about it.'

Ali felt her body flush with heat as she breathed heavily into the phone. There was an unbearable tingling between her legs and she pressed her bottom into the mattress to ease the deep-seated ache.

'Touch yourself,' he urged, remembering vividly how sweet she was. He gripped the sheet beside him to stop himself from ripping off the towel. 'Are you wet?' he asked, his voice so deep and rough he barely recognised it. 'Are you ready for me?'

Ali mindlessly followed his command. She quivered as her first tentative touch caused a pulse to throb to life deep inside.

'N-no,' she murmured as her light touch found her wanting.

'I don't believe you,' he murmured. 'I can hear it in your voice, Aleisha. You. Are. Ready.'

Ali hesitated. It had been many years since she'd done any kind of self-exploration and even with the devil himself whispering illicit instructions, urging her on, it felt...juvenile.

'Do it, Aleisha,' he growled, already picturing her pleasuring herself in his mind's eye. Already hearing her throaty cries as she orgasmed in his ear. 'You know you want to,' he added, dropping his voice another octave. 'You know you want to come. You know you want me to make you.'

Ali shivered. She did. God, help her, she did. She was going to hell, *no doubt about it*, but right now the dictates of her libido were drowning out all sense.

She slid her finger inside. Internal muscles contracted around her and an involuntary moan slipped from her mouth.

Ali shivered as her finger met the warm slick lubrication that Max craved. That she craved. 'Oh yes,' she half sighed, half moaned.

'I told you,' he whispered. 'I told you, you were ready for me. Now, touch your breasts again,' he ordered.

Ali mindlessly did his bidding, her still erect nipples flowering beneath her dewy touch.

'I want to taste them,' he half crooned, half groaned.

His admission, low and sweet, caused another deep contraction and Ali felt a surge of moisture at the apex of her thighs.

'I want you to taste them too,' she whispered. 'I want you to taste between my legs too.'

Max groaned into the phone as an image of him kneeling between her thighs paralysed him.

'Stroke yourself.' His husky command was

urgent. 'I want to hear you come. I want to hear you call my name as you come.'

Ali slid her hands back down. She was ready. Eager for her touch. Throbbing for release.

'Ah-h-h,' she cried as her sensitised flesh leapt to life at her first exploratory stroke.

'Yes,' Max whispered as her whimper got him harder still. 'Close your eyes. Pretend it's me. Me touching you, tasting you.'

Driven by his sexual rhetoric, Ali found the hard little nub she sought easily. She stroked it at his urging and it reared against her touch, painful in its sensitivity.

She almost orgasmed instantly. 'Ah-h-h,' she murmured.

'You like that? Can you feel me? I love how you taste.'

Ali cried out as the line between pleasure and pain blurred and the sensations overpowered her.

'Easy, Aleisha,' Max murmured, his voice low and steady. 'Take it easy. Don't rush. I like to go slow. I like to savour every little whimper, every little squirm.'

Ali instantly slowed the pace, eased back on the pressure. She sucked in a breath as the sensations dropped to a slow hum, a languorous buzz. A small whimper escaped as the maelstrom subsided and she could breathe.

Max heard the frantic edge to her indecipherable utterings lessen and the ratcheting tension in his neck and shoulders eased.

'That's good,' he crooned, desperately fighting to control the freight-train pace of his own breath. 'We have time, we have all night.'

Ali relaxed as he murmured sweet nothings in her ear. He told her how he wanted to kiss her all over. How he dreamt about her. How her vanilla scent drove him crazy and he'd fantasised about doing her on his desk in her skirt.

And soon the storm was on her again. But she was prepared for it now, had kept pace with its build and she welcomed the maelstrom with all its thunder and lightning.

'Oh, God, Max,' she moaned as she pushed away the first ripple.

'It's okay, Aleisha, you can let it go now.'

Ali shook her head, her eyes squeezed shut. No, she needed him to say her name. Her real name. 'Ali,' she snapped as she pushed away another ripple. 'It's Ali.'

Max shook his head. *Was she trying to kill him?* 'Damn it, Max,' Ali panted. 'Say it.'

'No,' he insisted.

Ali refused to come without hearing it. 'I'm not…' She slowed the pace. 'I won't…'

Max set his jaw. 'Yes, you are. Yes, you will.'

Slowing the pace didn't work. Her body was already spiralling. 'Max!'

Max heard the growing desperation and knew she was close. 'It's too late, Aleisha, you're there,' he goaded, hanging onto his last skerrick of restraint.

'No...I won't,' she insisted as a pulse started to spread from her fingers out. She shook her head, ignoring the dark warning in his voice, fighting the pull.

'Come, Aleisha,'

'No.' *Damn it, no.*

Max could feel his chest pounding, his breath bursting in his lungs. She was fighting it. Fighting her own orgasm. Fighting the one thing he could give her—the only thing.

'Let go, Aleisha, let go.'

'Damn it, Max,' she cried out because she was almost there and she couldn't hold it back any longer, she wanted it too much and she simply wasn't strong enough to hold out against him.

Another thing she couldn't control.

Max recognised surrender when he heard it. 'Yes,' he breathed. 'Yes, *Ali*, yes.'

His rough, almost pained words reached her through the haze delivering what she'd craved on a broken whisper. 'Max,' she panted as she broke into a thousand pieces.

Max gripped the phone as Ali's cries reached an ear-shattering crescendo. They vibrated down the line directly into his brain, twisting like a tornado through every cell in his body.

Torturing, tormenting, teasing.

Even as they eased, dropping to low throaty whimpers, they taunted him with their passionate intensity. Right in his ear she seemed so close.

Touchable. Real. Concrete.

As if she were in bed beside him.

Ali slowly spun back to earth, sucking in frantic breaths, grappling to understand what she'd just allowed to happen as her hands fell uselessly on the bed beside her and her bones turned to liquid. 'Max...I...' she panted. 'That was...'

Max heard the confusion in her breathy voice. 'It's okay,' he murmured. 'I know.'

He knew? *Did he do this often?* 'But, I...'

She what? She couldn't think. *Hell, she could barely breathe!* 'You called me Ali,' she murmured, because it had whispered into her ear at just the right moment and ricocheted around her head echoing to the time of her orgasm.

He grimaced at his slip, annoyed at himself for succumbing. But her cries had pushed him to the edge and it had seemed like the most natural thing in the world to do.

'It's okay, Max,' she yawned as his silence stretched. 'It was just what I needed.'

Max should have been pleased that he'd given her what she needed but his body was aching, his honour was dented and her voice in his ear was just too damn much. 'Go to sleep, Aleisha. Sweet dreams.'

It took Ali a moment to realise the phone had gone dead and she stared at it for a while before she hit the end button.

She was asleep in under a minute.

Max, still awake at four a.m., finally admitted defeat and hit the pavements again.

Ali met up with Reginald Aimes the next morning on her way into court and they were chatting in the foyer waiting for the rest of the team when Max approached from behind. Ali blushed as he greeted her, their telephonic tryst from last night still making her hot all over.

She was nervous too in her deliberately provocative clothes. Last night she'd selfishly taken what was on offer from him. This morning she wanted to show him what was on offer from her.

Max studiously avoided looking at anything other than her eyes. The back view of that banned sexy skirt combined with sheer black stockings, stilettos and white clingy blouse he could definitely make out her bra strap through had been enough of a jolt.

His air-hostess fantasy given form and shape.

He wouldn't give her the satisfaction of checking out the front view in front of Reg. 'You look...well rested,' he commented politely as a cloud of vanilla enveloped him and his libido growled.

Ali kept her face neutral. 'Thanks, I had some...help.'

Max quirked an eyebrow. 'You took my advice about a sleeping pill?'

She shook her head. 'Apparently there are other more... alternative ways, to get off to sleep.'

Max's lips twitched. 'Massage, deep breathing...something like that?'

Ali pressed her lips together as his husky commanding whisper from last night revisited. Her skin goosed. She was acutely aware of Reg beside her ignorant to the subtext.

She nodded. 'Something like that.'

Reg's phone rang and he excused himself. Max glanced over his shoulder then back to her, allowing his gaze free rein. He shook his head. 'Seriously, Aleisha? That skirt? The vanilla.' He kept his voice low. 'Are you trying to drive me insane?'

'I think that's only fair after last night,' she murmured.

Max felt his resolve to make a clean break weaken. 'It's working.'

Aleisha smiled. 'I'm also not wearing any underwear.'

It had seemed a rather daring thing to do this morning as she was dressing but it had been sufficiently titillating to distract her from the day ahead and anything that could do that was a good thing as far as she was concerned.

Max narrowed his gaze as his resolve disappeared into the fires of damnation right along with his soul.

To hell with ending it—he could do that tomorrow.

'So, you're feeling better today?'

Ali quirked an eyebrow at the sudden gravelly quality of his tone. 'Rested. Very rested.'

And more than a little resigned. Yesterday had been nerve-wracking—today was a complete anticlimax.

'Good, because when we walk out of this courtroom in an hour or so—win or lose—you and I are going straight to bed. And don't expect to be getting out of it any time soon.'

Ali swallowed as lust rolled through her belly like a giant Mexican wave.

It took Judge Davies twenty minutes to sum up the case and hand down her finding that Brisbane Memorial and Dr Aleisha Gregory had no case to answer in the death of Nathaniel Cullen.

Ali, who had been holding herself erect in her chair for the entire time it took her to get there, suddenly sagged as everyone around her leapt to their feet and erupted in cheers and applause.

It was over. It was truly over.

Somebody grabbed her by the elbow and yanked her up and hugged her, then someone else did the same and a third person pecked her on the cheek.

Max stood in front of her, the last to pass on his congratulations. 'We won.' He grinned.

Ali nodded, her heart filling with relief, vindication, gratitude, and something else that seemed too complex to even analyse right at that moment.

'Thank you.' She smiled. 'Thank you.'

She looked over at Nathaniel Cullen's parents. They were sobbing quietly, their lawyer talking to them in hushed tones, and her joy at being exonerated lost a little of its sparkle.

The bottom line was an eighteen-year-old boy was dead—there weren't any winners here.

But then people were chatting around her about an immediate lifting of her suspension and contacting the medical registration board to push along her start-back date and press releases and she was being swept out of the courtroom as everyone talked at once.

Max found her in the middle of the huddle five minutes later.

'Excuse me, gentlemen,' he said, grabbing her hand. 'Aleisha will be taking the weekend off to think about her next steps. Reg, she'll be in on Monday morning to talk to you—my secretary will set up an appointment.'

And then he pulled her out of the crowd, his fingers interwoven with hers, and stalked away with her. He let go of her hand a few moments later as he approached the lift and jabbed the down button. Then he fished in his pocket for his mobile and flipped it open.

'Valerie?' he said, his gaze capturing Ali's as he spoke. 'Tell Helen to cancel my appointments for today and reschedule. I'm going to be unavailable.'

He paused, obviously listening to something Valerie was saying, and Ali's mouth went dry at his predatory gleam.

'Yes,' he said, his eyes holding hers. 'All day. And I *do not* wish to be disturbed.'

The ancient lift dinged as it arrived and Ali stepped in as Max ended the call. Max stepped in also. The lift was empty and he took up position beside her.

The second the doors shut he dropped his briefcase, turned to face her, then dragged her close until she was squashed against him. He swooped his head down and plundered her soft mouth just as he had fantasised about last night. Her tiny whimper inflamed him and he walked her backwards, pressing her against the wall.

Their ragged breathing was loud in the silence as the kiss careened out of control.

His fingers grasped the material of her skirt and hitched it up one thigh. His hand took over, pushing beneath the tight fabric feeling the curve of silk clad female thigh beneath. His hand hit lace and he changed direction, moving to the back of her thigh, skimming bare flesh now as his palm slid further north.

And then he hit pay dirt.

One naked buttock filled his hand and he groaned against her mouth. 'You really don't have any underwear on, do you?'

Ali sucked in a breath, her head spinning, her hands clasped to his jacket lapels as her body clamoured for his hand to go further. She gave a half laugh. 'Did you think I was lying?'

He squeezed the gloriously naked flesh in his hand. 'I was hoping you weren't,' he murmured as he nuzzled her neck, sucking in her vanilla essence.

The lift bumped to the ground and they pulled apart. Thankfully the lift took its usual extended time to open giving Max time to step back and pick up his briefcase and Ali time to yank down her skirt.

By the time the doors finally opened they were standing apart staring straight ahead, all business. Only a very close observer would have noticed the unevenness of their breath.

'My car,' Max said as he strode out of the lift. 'Follow me.'

Ten minutes later Ali had been deposited in Max's sporty car in the darkened surrounds of the underground car park, waiting for him to join her. The scent of worn leather, the feel of it—like her favourite pair of kid gloves— against the backs of her thighs and the aroma of man, of Max, surrounded her.

She felt her pulse slow as a heavy sensation she was fast coming to recognise as lust stirred in her belly. He opened his door and she watched as his thigh came into view and the sensation liquefied into a surge of molten heat.

And so when he said, 'I thought that was an excellent result,' she lunged at him before he even had the chance to start the car, just as he had done in the lift, opening her mouth against his, thrusting her tongue as she moaned against his lips.

Then suddenly he muttered an expletive and she was hauled onto his lap, straddling his thighs in her impossibly tight skirt, his hands ploughing beneath the fabric, past her lace-tops, pushing the skirt higher and higher until he was grasping both of her naked buttocks in his hands.

She reached for his tie as they devoured each other's mouths, sliding it out of his collar with a satisfying zip. His buttons were next and she managed to get a few undone before one of his hands wandered to the apex of her thighs and stroked.

Her breath hissed out and her back arched as his finger found just the right spot.

Max took advantage of her bared neck and latched on to the pulse that beat a frantic tattoo at the base of her throat. His arm hit the gear stick, his knee bashed against the centre console and anyone could come along at any minute and spot the great Max Sherrington making out in his car with a former witness, but cream puffs and macaroons infused his senses and he gorged like a starving man.

He laved her neck and she tasted every bit as sweet as she gasped and mewed in response.

Ali could barely think as his finger stroked deep inside her but she knew she wanted more. She'd been there done that last night, right now she wanted the real thing, so she reached for his zipper without conscious thought, satisfied to find him hard against her fingers, aroused as she was.

Max groaned against her neck as her fingers brushed his erection through his trousers. He couldn't ever remember being this hard—not even last night as every nuance of her orgasm had been delivered directly into his ear.

He heard his zip give, loud even amidst their combined frantic breath. Felt her fingers on him, questing for a way to be closer.

He cried out against her neck when she found it. Her palm clamping around him— squeezing, milking. Flesh on flesh.

He wanted that too. To be closer. Wanted to feel her tight around him. To touch every inch of her. One hand abandoned the slick heat of her, needing to touch her breasts. He'd lived vicariously last night but not any more.

He fumbled with her buttons as she stroked him, needing to feel them, see them, taste them.

Ali revelled in the feel of him in her hand, thick and strong. But she needed more. She needed him in her. Last night, as she had touched herself at his command, she had fantasised about him stroking deep inside her but she didn't have to imagine now.

She could have.

'Max,' she cried as he pushed her partially undone blouse as far down her arms as it would go and she ground down against him.

Max felt her glide along the length of him as

he yanked a bra cup aside and sucked heavily on an engorged nipple.

Ali threw her head back, her cry reverberating around the car. She lifted herself slightly, positioning him for entry.

'No, Ali, wait...' Max panted, some skerrick of sanity rearing its head amidst the maelstrom at just the right moment. 'Condom,' he panted.

Ali almost wept at his words. She needed him inside her. They were a whisper away from it.

How could she have forgotten about condoms?

She bit her lip, forced herself to stop grinding against the hard, hard length of him.

'Have you got one?' she panted.

Max squeezed his eyes shut, his fingers stilling then dropping away from her, gripping the outside of her thighs instead. 'No. They're at home.'

Ali stared at him for a long moment, their heaving chests and erratic breathing in sync. She bit her lip.

'Bloody hell,' she panted before awkwardly easing off him to sit in her own seat, trying to pull her skirt down and return her bared breasts to the confines of her bra.

Max also fixed himself up with shaking fingers, giving his breathing a chance to return to normal.

'How far to your place?' she asked.

Max's gaze dropped to her still unbuttoned blouse. 'Fifteen minutes.'

Ali looked him square in the eye. 'How fast if I don't do this up?'

He feasted his eyes on the white lacy bra cups. 'Ten.'

She nodded. 'I'll let you do whatever you want with them if you can get us there faster.'

Max made it home in eight minutes flat.

CHAPTER TEN

THE sky was just starting to lighten when Max woke early Sunday morning. He glanced over to Ali. She was lying on her stomach with her head turned away. One thigh stuck out from the sheet that barely covered her bottom.

His lazy gaze followed the long stretch of naked skin from where the sheet ended to the graceful dip forming the small of her back and up the gentle rise of her ribcage to the flat expanse of her shoulder blades.

And he wanted her again.

It would be so easy to run his palm up the contours of her back, drop a kiss on her shoulder, whisper his intentions in her ear just as if he had the last two days and nights. He could picture her sleepy smile now as she rolled over and snuggled all her warm female curves against him.

He even lifted his hand to do just that.

But the longer she stayed in his bed, the more times he reached for her, the more he wanted her. And after eighteen months on his own, it was a trifle alarming to think how quickly she'd become part of his world.

Two days ago he'd planned to make a swift break.

Now his whole damn bedroom smelled of vanilla. He was never going to be able to get rid of it.

He dropped his hand.

The same had happened with Tori. She'd just always been there. And look how disastrously that had turned out.

Maybe it was time to practise a little restraint? Get a little perspective?

He eased out of bed, careful not to wake her as he padded to his en suite and changed into his jogging clothes. Nothing like a brisk morning jog for clarity.

Ali stirred the moment Max vacated the bed, as if some sixth sense had woken her. She rolled over, reaching for him. When her questing hands came up wanting she cracked open an eyelid.

She almost mewed her disappointment.

Noises from the en suite were reassuring however and she dragged the sheet up all the way up to her armpits to cover her cool skin. Her eyes fluttered closed. Her body ached in a good way and she smiled to herself at the things they'd done to cause it.

Ali heard Max re-enter the bedroom and she opened her eyes. 'Morning,' she murmured as he appeared in his exercise gear, joggers clasped in one hand.

He glanced at her and his groin tightened. 'Sorry, I didn't mean to wake you.'

Ali raised an eyebrow. 'Doesn't seem to have bothered you before now.'

Max chuckled as he sat on the side of the bed to put on his joggers.

'You're going for a run?' She glanced at the clock. 'At this hour?'

'You're not a morning person, are you?' he said as he pulled on a sock.

Ali shrugged. 'I'm a shift worker. When we get the chance to sleep in the dark we take it.'

But then of course she realised she wasn't any more. A shift worker. She really needed to stop thinking of herself as one.

Max pulled his joggers on and tied them up, steadfastly ignoring her very tempting presence behind him. He stood and turned. 'I can bring back some croissants for breakfast if you like? And the Sunday papers?'

Ali let her gaze wander up and down the magnificent length of him as he looked down at her, hands on hips. His thighs were moulded perfectly in the skins he was wearing. His broad shoulders, flat abdomen and smooth tanned biceps were beautifully displayed in his white singlet shirt with last year's Gold Coast Marathon advertised upon it.

Her breasts grew heavy. Heat spiralled in her belly.

'Did you know,' she murmured, 'that you burn off the same amount of calories during sex as you do during a five-k run?'

Max felt his breath hitch as she all but licked her lips as she looked him up and down. He felt completely objectified.

He really, really shouldn't have been so turned on by it.

He dug his fingers into his hips. 'I do ten.'

Ali smiled as she peeled the sheet back. 'Okay, then. I'll let you do me twice.'

Max swallowed hard as she flashed him her naked reclined body in all its glory. He toed off his shoes and stripped his shirt off over his head in a matter of seconds.

Forget clarity.

Several hours later they were on his deck drinking coffee and reading the Sunday papers. His penthouse suite overlooked the Brisbane River and the sun glittered on the surface below. A light breeze ruffled the edge of the newspapers.

Ali glanced up through her fringe at a bare-chested Max. She was wearing his gown and her feet were in his lap snuggled up against his cotton boxers. He was absently rubbing her arch as he perused the sports section of the paper.

Her heart did a little flop in her chest. It smacked of domesticity and Ali couldn't remember being this contented in a long time. With the stress of the case behind her and the shiny new possibilities ahead, it had been an excellent couple of days.

Tomorrow was Monday and everything would no doubt change. Max would go to work and she had to figure out what to do with the rest of her life. So she'd take this moment of domesticity for what it was and worry about tomorrow tomorrow.

Max looked up and caught her watching him and smiled at her. 'I checked my messages while you were in the shower,' he said, his hands straying from her ankle to her calf and then back down again.

He couldn't believe he'd gone nearly forty-eight hours without checking his messages. He never did that. But then he'd never been quite so thoroughly distracted.

'Helen rang on Friday to say she booked an eleven a.m. appointment for you with Reg tomorrow.'

Ali grimaced. *Tomorrow.* There was that word again.

Max waited for Ali to answer. When she said

nothing he asked, 'Have you thought about how soon you'll return?'

Ali sighed. He just didn't get that she really wasn't going back.

'Let's not talk about it, Max, please. Thanks to you I'm having a fun couple of days away from the real world. Just you and me. And it's okay,' she hastened to add in case he thought she was already picking out china patterns, 'I know it's not what either of us need in our lives and it's nothing serious. I know it's nothing more than two adults having some fun. But, we've both had a terrible year, I think we've earned a little fun, don't you?'

Max nodded. He couldn't agree more. 'Absolutely.'

She smiled. 'Good. For a moment there I thought I might have to take this gown off and distract you again.'

He grinned. 'Don't let me stop you.'

Heat licked quick and intense between them and her nipples pebbled against the soft terry towelling. Ali dropped her hand to the knot and watched as Max's gaze followed her movements—undoing the tie, opening the lapels a little and then a little more until her naked breasts were bared to his gaze and the soft morning sunshine.

Max licked his lips as her large breasts with

perfect nipples sat bare and exposed for his own private viewing.

Him and anyone else out on their balconies on a beautiful Sunday morning with a pair of binoculars.

He leaned closer to her. 'Perfect,' he murmured.

A loud knock on the door halted his progress and he muttered an expletive.

Ali grinned. 'Saved by the bell.'

He shook his head. 'Don't move a muscle,' he ordered as he stood. 'It's probably just a courier with some papers.' Another sharp rap came from the direction of the front door.

'Later,' she murmured, securing the robe.

He dropped a brief hard kiss on her mouth. 'Tease.'

Ali smiled at him as he strutted away, his black boxers clinging to him like a second skin. She sighed at the perfection of him and then returned her attention to the book-review section.

Max swaggered into the kitchen and headed towards the door with a smile on his face, his early morning doubts behind him. Ali seemed to be on the same page as him. A weekend of fun. No strings. No promises. No commitments.

A perfect weekend.

Except for Pete, who was standing on the doorstep when Max opened the door.

Pete took one look at his friend's state of dress and quirked an eyebrow. 'Well, well, well,' he murmured.

'Go away,' Max ordered, attempting to shut the door.

Pete chuckled. 'Not for a million bucks.' He grinned, his forearm blocking the door's closure as he angled his body inside the apartment.

'Well, what do we have here?' Pete asked as his gaze strayed to the partially obscured deck where he could just see a decidedly female hand cradled around a mug.

'Nothing.'

Max didn't know what this thing between him and Ali was. And he resented Pete's appearance, forcing him to define it. He felt the disquiet he'd woken with this morning revisit. What were they doing?

And was he ready for it?

'Pete,' Max warned as his friend headed for the deck.

But Pete did what he always did—exactly as he pleased—and he was standing in front of Ali in less than ten seconds.

'Hello, Pete,' Ali greeted, trying to keep it light but wishing the ground would swallow her. Wishing that the real world hadn't intruded into her weekend fantasy world.

Max sighed as he pulled up behind his friend. 'You remember Ali, Pete?'

'But of course.' Pete beamed. 'Ali, Ali, Ali... how are you? I see you won the court case.'

Ali nodded. 'With a little help from my...'

She glanced at Max. What was he exactly? *Her lawyer?*

Standing beside her in his underwear?

Damn Pete for his intrusion, for forcing her to ask all those questions she was putting off for the weeks ahead. 'Friends.'

Max could see Ali disappearing into the shell she'd been humping around when he first met her. 'Was there something you wanted... *mate*?'

Pete grinned, looking from one to the other, unperturbed. 'Ah, yep, but you're obviously... otherwise engaged so it can wait.'

'Excellent,' Max said, clamping a hand on Pete's shoulder.

'No, no,' Ali said, standing. 'You guys hang out for a bit. I'll make myself scarce.'

Max opened his mouth to protest but Ali was already picking up dishes off the table and heading into the kitchen. He turned to Pete with exasperation and noticed his friend checking out Ali's very delectable sway.

He clenched his teeth. 'Don't even think about it.'

Pete was taken aback by the sinister tone

in his friend's voice. Max was using his court voice. And frankly it had always scared the bejeebers out of him.

Ali must mean something.

Which was just as well given the news he had to impart.

'So…you and Ali,' Pete said as Ali stepped into the apartment and out of earshot.

'What do you want?' Max demanded.

'Oh, come on, Maxy, throw me a bone. What's she like?'

Max thought back to their sexual feast over the last couple of days with absolutely no intention of sharing any of it.

'She's hell on my training schedule,' he dismissed with a cryptic smile. 'Now…What. Do. You. Want?'

Pete hesitated. 'I found something out this morning that I think you're not going to like. So I wanted you to hear it from me. I think you may need to sit down.'

Ali hadn't planned on eavesdropping. But the window near the sink faced the deck and it was already open, the men's voices carrying easily on the light morning breeze as they sat at the table.

'Okay. I'm sitting. Now what?'

Pete fished his mobile out of his pocket. 'I was online this morning. Tori posted a status update.'

Max frowned. He didn't care about social media. Or Tori. 'I thought Tori unfriended you?'

Pete shook his head. 'No. Just you.'

Max sighed. 'What is it?'

Pete paused for a moment to decide if there was some way to soften the blow. He handed the phone over to Max, open on Tori's social network page. 'She's pregnant.'

Max stared at the gadget in his hands, not quite comprehending for a moment even after he read the gushing update.

It's official—I'm pregnant. It's amazing how it all falls into place when you meet the right man. I haven't been this happy in a very long time. I love you baby. Both of you.

'You okay?' Pete asked.

Max clenched his jaw. Tori was pregnant. Tori, who didn't want babies, was pregnant.

And apparently ecstatic about it.

He remembered back to their one and only pregnancy scare. How angry she'd been, how indignant. How certain she'd been that she didn't want the potential new life that might have been growing inside her.

Her threats to have an abortion.

His hand tightened on the phone as he glanced at Pete without saying a word.

Ali didn't dare breathe as she stood at the sink. Max's rigid profile sucked the marrow from her bones.

He *was* still in love with his wife.

It was as plain as the nose on her face.

But that wasn't the worst of it. The truly horrible thing was she loved him. She'd actually fallen for him.

And...*he was still in love with his wife.*

Pete watched as his friend's knuckles whitened around his expensive new phone and wondered for a moment if Max was going to shatter the screen.

'She was a bitch, Max. She didn't deserve you.'

'She wasn't, Pete,' Max said, his voice controlled as he handed back the phone.

Max knew that he'd spent a good chunk of the last eighteen months hating Tori—for the affair, for leaving, for denying him a shot at being a father. But he also knew she'd essentially been a good person. He wouldn't have fallen for her if she hadn't been. The truth was, they hadn't wanted the same things and he'd always known it deep down inside.

'She just...didn't want *my* babies.'

Ali felt as if she'd taken a hammer blow to the middle of her chest at the lament in Max's words. She'd expected anger. She remembered the pain of Tom's betrayal—how deep it had cut—and Max had been betrayed doubly.

Instead she detected regret and loneliness and resignation.

And her heart broke. For him. And for her. She'd already loved one man who had ditched her for another; she wasn't stupid enough to make that mistake again.

She had to get out of here!

Pete was heading back out of the door when he ran into a fully dressed Ali searching the lounge room for her handbag she vaguely remembered discarding somewhere between the door and the bedroom.

'You're leaving?' he said, taking in her change of clothes.

Ali looked down at the outfit she'd worn into court on Friday morning and tried not to look guilty. 'Yes.'

'You heard?'

Ali nodded. 'Yes.'

'Please don't. He's going to need you today. Can you be here for him?'

Ali shut her eyes to block out the painful truth. *Even Pete thought he was still in love with Tori.* Pete, his best friend, the man who knew Max probably better than anyone else.

She nodded. 'Sure.'

'Promise?'

Ali nodded.

Even though she knew it was a promise she had no intention of keeping. There was absolutely no way she could stay a second longer than was necessary. Her heart had had enough trampling this past year, she needed to guard it as best she could from any further damage. If she walked away now and never looked back maybe it was just possible.

A quick goodbye and she was out of here.

Max was still on the deck when Ali joined him a few minutes later. He was staring out over the river, a frown furrowing his forehead. He didn't even seem to notice the tap of her heels against the wooden decking that echoed loudly into the tranquil morning air.

'Max?'

Max dragged his gaze away from the river and his turbulent thoughts. Ali stood fully dressed before him in that skirt, her butterscotch curls brushing the see-through blouse, and a sudden fierce welling of desire crashed like a tsunami through his system.

It was totally unexpected in his current state of turmoil. And utterly welcome.

Twenty minutes ago he'd resented Pete for making him examine what the hell he and Ali were doing.

Now it was clear.

Ali was who he wanted. Ali was who mattered.

He stood abruptly, the scraping of his chair ringing across the river. He took three paces towards her and hauled her into his arms, swooping his head, crushing his mouth to hers.

Her instant response was gratifying and he groaned as he grabbed both her butt cheeks and jammed her up against his hard raging body. He pulled at her blouse, unzipped her skirt.

Ali held onto him for dear life as her head spun and her insides turned to liquid.

'Max,' she panted, pulling away, her eyes shutting as his mouth moved to devour her neck. She was pretty sure Pete hadn't meant to be there for Max like this. 'Do you want to talk about this?'

Max ran his tongue over her ear lobe. He didn't want to talk. He just wanted to feel. To bury himself in her. Get lost in her essence. Just be with her. He wished he didn't want it so much. But he did. 'No.'

Ali gripped his biceps as his hot, desperate kisses eroded her determination to flee. She reached for a modicum of common sense in a rapidly diminishing world. 'I know what it's like, Max. To want a baby. To have that taken from you.'

'No talking,' he muttered against her neck

as he yanked a bra cup aside and claimed her breast with his palm.

A surge of lust pounded through Ali's veins as his thumb stroked her nipple and she cried out. It washed through her brain crippling everything but the imperative to kiss back.

Long, deep, wet and hard.

Open-mouthed.

As good as she was getting. Better.

Obliterating everything. Making her forget. About Tori and the baby. About her promise to Pete. About her deep-and-getting-deeper-every-second love for him.

About practically fornicating in full public view on his deck.

And then he was kissing her again and lifting her up and carrying her, not breaking their lip lock or his stride as he blindly navigated the inside of the apartment. Suddenly she was horizontal on his bed, sucking in much-needed air as she watched him strip off underwear that was barely concealing him.

She should stop him, have more pride. Was it even her he was making love to? But she wanted him too fiercely, was powerless to resist the thrum in her blood and the love in her heart.

Powerless to deny him this outlet.

And too selfish not to take whatever of himself was on offer.

Because after today, she'd only have the memories.

With no underwear and her skirt ruched up around her hips she was totally bare to his fiery gaze.

She spread her legs in silent invitation.

Max grabbed a condom from the very well used box and was sliding into her moist heat within seconds. He groaned into her neck and let the wild impulsive rhythm playing in his head take control.

Ali, her clothes still askew, slipped out of the bed half an hour later. Max had drifted to sleep almost immediately and she'd been content to cuddle up close and listen to his breath, mentally cataloguing every husky nuance.

But it was time to go. She'd given up being a victim in court on Friday and she wouldn't leave herself open to it again.

She was a survivor. She could do it.

Her breath caught on a sob as a sudden rush of loss stabbed like a hot knife between her ribs.

Could she? Could she really?

How much loss could a human being take? How much more could she bear? Max. Nathaniel Cullen. Tom. Her baby.

The knife twisted viciously. God, she'd been so caught up in winning and being with Max she'd forgotten she'd promised herself she'd grieve her baby's passing after the case.

Her tiny, defenceless baby. The small but potent life force that she'd known for only a few short weeks.

The pain and the anguish of that horrible day drove the knife a little deeper and Ali stifled a sob. She pressed her palm against her belly, where her baby had grown. It felt so empty and the ache inside that had been there for a year intensified.

She looked down at a sleeping Max and her vision blurred. He'd lost a baby too. It might not have been conceived yet but, if his devastated face earlier was any indication, he'd wanted a baby as badly as she had.

Her heart felt as if it were cracking wide open. How much loss could it stand? First her baby and now the man she'd foolishly fallen in love with.

The man she loved, loved another.

Ali felt herself crumpling from the inside. She had to get out of here. She whirled away, strode out of his door and didn't look back.

CHAPTER ELEVEN

A WEEK passed, two, since Max had woken to an empty bed and a note on his kitchen bench. Ali had thanked him for the weekend and then left him in no doubt that it was all it was ever going to be. They were both still too raw from their previous relationships to be anything more than transient distractions, she'd written. And she had a life to get back on track. She didn't need any diversions while she was doing it.

Which was fine. Perfectly fine.

He just hadn't expected to miss her this much.

In the middle of a court case he'd suddenly realise he was thinking about her instead of listening to the proceedings. Or at home each night he realised he was waiting for the phone to ring. Itching to pick it up himself, hear her voice as she rattled off her next hare-brained career scheme.

And then there was the bedroom. Vanilla permeated his sheets and haunted his macaroon dreams. His towels carried the scent, even his shower.

She was everywhere and he missed her.

It wasn't the same as the way he'd missed Tori, either. In fact he'd been too angry to miss her and, if he was being honest, somewhere deep down there had been a small sense of relief.

But all there was now was a constant heavy feeling inside his chest.

He kept hoping an excuse would come up to ring her or see her. Anything...

And then in the third week his prayers were answered and he wished like hell he could take them back.

Notification of the lodgment of an appeal against the findings in the wrongful death suit against Brisbane Memorial Hospital and Dr Aleisha Gregory landed in his in-tray.

His heart sank as he read the documentation. *Anything but this.*

It had always been a possibility, they'd known that, but he hadn't thought the Cullens would go through with it.

He stared at the papers for hours wishing it weren't his way back to Ali. But she had to be told.

And he didn't want it to come from anyone else.

Max jogged along the darkened Southbank pathway later that night on his way to the River

Breeze café. At almost ten on a Tuesday night the place was nearly deserted as restaurants and outdoor eateries wound up their trade.

He didn't even know what he was doing here. He hadn't planned on telling her tonight at all. But the longer he sat with the news alone in his apartment, the more it felt like a ticking bomb.

In the end, he couldn't stand keeping it to himself any longer. He rang her home number and got no answer. He rang the River Breeze and got Kat who—thankfully—informed him that Ali was working until close. He'd left his apartment immediately, deciding an extra run would be good for his training schedule.

Thirty minutes later he was almost there and he slowed his pace as the lights of the River Breeze came into view. Unfortunately, despite grappling with the words all the way here, he wasn't any closer to finding the right ones.

Some lawyer he was if he couldn't even articulate a very simple concept without tying himself in a knot.

He paused outside, stretching out his legs on the bottom of four steps that led into the café, catching his breath, wanting to go in, desperate to see her and yet not under these circumstances.

Not wanting to be the portent of doom.

He almost changed his mind. Turned around

and ran all the way back home. He could get Helen to ring her tomorrow during business hours, set up an appointment. But then the glass doors opened and he caught a glimpse of her and her butterscotch curls bouncing by and he knew he couldn't put it off any longer.

Ali was wiping down a table when the hairs on the back of her neck prickled and she turned to identify the cause even though, deep inside somewhere, she already knew.

He stood before her in his jogging gear looking warm and male and vital and her gaze devoured him. He looked as he had that morning she'd persuaded him to use her for his morning workout and it had been two weeks since she'd kissed him and every cell in her body was screaming.

'Max,' she said, hating the breathiness of her voice.

'Hi.'

It was another moment or two before Ali realised they were standing like statues staring at each other. His gaze felt like a white-hot laser as it grazed her breasts and her thighs and her belly and her body bloomed with heat.

Kat bustled by and Ali gained some cerebral function. 'Would you like a table?' she asked.

Max shook his head. She was all business in her tight black T-shirt, black trousers and long maroon apron emblazoned with a River Breeze logo. 'I'd like to talk to you.'

Ali felt her silly heart leap in her chest before she ruthlessly crushed it. The man was still in love with his ex-wife—what else was there to talk about?

'I'm busy,' she said stiffly because she couldn't bear to be this near to him and yet feel so far away.

Max looked around at the half-full café seemingly oblivious to their exchange. He shrugged. 'I can wait.'

Ali felt suddenly churlish as he stood there calmly looking at her. She'd meant what she'd said in her note—why didn't he just let her get on with it?

'Suit yourself,' she said and left him standing as she returned to the kitchen. To her job. Her very simple, non-stress, non-critical job.

Over the next half-hour Max sat and watched Ali as she flitted between tables. She laughed and joked, chatted, cleared away, took orders and generally seemed to fulfil the role of waitress very efficiently. But when he watched her examine a customer's leg and then go away and come back with some kind of cream in a tube he couldn't help but roll his eyes.

It was plain to all but her, apparently, that she had a true calling and being a waitress was never going to be a fulfilling career choice.

Finally, with all but two tables empty, she approached him with a couple of steaming coffee cups in hand. She plonked one in front of him and took the seat opposite. The aroma of Arabica beans enveloped him and Max watched as she stirred sugar into her coffee, waiting for her to say something.

Ali placed the spoon on the saucer and finally lifted her gaze to his. 'What do you want, Max?'

Max opened his mouth to tell her, to say *they're appealing,* but he shied away from the directness of it all. His gaze searched her face. She seemed weary and he wondered if she was getting as little sleep as him.

'I've missed you,' he murmured.

Ali's pulse kicked up a notch, her heart threatening to fly at the encouraging comment, but her head remained stubbornly level. 'Is that what you came to tell me?'

He paused. No, it wasn't, but it didn't make it any less true. 'I—'

A sudden commotion—a plate smashing, a woman crying out—interrupted what he'd been about to say and both he and Ali turned to identify the source of the intrusion. A group of people were huddled around a man on the ground who appeared to be having a seizure.

'Ali!' Kat called as she rushed from behind

the cash register towards the table of uni students who'd been celebrating a birthday.

But Ali was already on her feet, moving towards the emergency, Max hot on her heels.

'What's happening?' a woman wailed.

'He'll swallow his tongue—here, put this spoon in his mouth,' someone else said.

'It's okay,' Ali said, her voice permeating the panic that had erupted as people at the table all reacted at once. 'Step aside,' she urged, a natural authority in her voice as she removed the spoon from the offending hand and pushed her way into the huddle. 'I'm a doctor.'

She got down on the floor beside the flailing young man and turned his head to the side while lifting his jaw a little to prevent his tongue from blocking his airway.

'Max, can you time the duration of the fit, please?' she asked. 'Kat, get my bag.' She smiled at the nearest girl, who was crying. 'It's okay—he's having a seizure but it shouldn't last too long. Clear some space for him so he doesn't hurt himself. Does he have epilepsy?' she asked.

There was a collective no. 'He did play football earlier today and got crunched pretty bad in a tackle,' one of the party admitted. 'He was out of it for a few seconds.'

Ali kept her smile firmly in place despite

the alarming news. 'Max, call an ambulance please.'

Max flipped out his phone and dialled. By the time he got through to triple zero the seizure had stopped and Ali was putting the young man into the recovery position. She calmly soothed everyone's frazzled nerves and explained that Josh, as he was called, would be very sleepy for a while as she shone a penlight she'd extracted from her bag into Josh's eyes.

Fortunately it was only minutes before the sound of a siren rent the air and two paramedics arrived on the scene. Max watched Ali as she worked in tandem with the paramedics, inserting a drip and getting a drowsy Josh onto the gurney while rattling off a lot of medical jargon.

It was now, right in this moment, watching her work methodically and efficiently, utterly engaged with the situation, that he finally got how devastating the Cullen case must have been to her.

How devastating the news of an appeal would be.

Working with medico-legal cases had blinded him to the emotional impact on the individuals working at the coalface. For him it was simple—in this big, bad, litigious world, doctors got sued. It was just the way it was now. And should be something every doctor prepared for.

But if Ali gave her all to every patient as she was right now, to Josh, a complete stranger—and watching her, how could he believe anything else?—then Nathaniel Cullen's death would have been a personal tragedy to her too.

Dr Aleisha Gregory was one hell of a doctor and he finally understood how much it must have damaged her to have had it snatched away.

How scary it would be to return after being ripped to shreds.

How gutting the appeal was going to be.

The ambulance departed in a screaming hurry fifteen minutes later and Ali watched from the bottom step of the café entrance as the red strobing became more distant. She rubbed at her arms as the adrenaline that had kept her sharp and focused dissipated, leaving her cold and shaky.

Still she hadn't felt this alive, this engaged, this…right…in a long time.

Max watched her from the café's open glass doors staring at the disappearing ambulance. After a moment he joined her, coming to a halt on the step behind. He placed his hands on her shoulders, then tentatively took over the rubbing action.

He expected her to protest, but when her hands fell to her sides he became bolder, rubbing briskly. They didn't say anything for a while, just watched the diminishing lights.

'Will he be okay?' Max asked when the lights finally faded.

She shrugged. 'Depends…if it's just concussion, sure, if it's something more serious… It's too hard to tell without looking at CT scans.'

Max applied gentle pressure to her arms and turned her around until he was looking down into her face. 'Are you okay?'

Ali felt a rush of love at his gentle enquiry. It bloomed in her chest like a mushroom cloud. 'Sure,' she said, swallowing hard against the block of emotion threatening to clog her throat.

As okay as she was ever going to be.

Max felt the raw, husky timbre of her voice reach right inside him. He pushed back that unruly curl flopping in her eye, lightly brushing her forehead as he went. It was gratifying to see her sway slightly towards him as she shut her eyes.

'You were awesome tonight,' he murmured.

Ali's eyes fluttered open. 'I did what anyone would have done,' she dismissed.

Max shook his head. 'No, Ali. You did what a doctor would do.'

Ali knew he was right. Knew that she was a doctor right down to her DNA. Knew that nothing she ever did would beat saving people's lives.

And it scared her witless.

To her complete and utter horror, she burst into tears.

'Hey, hey.' Max frowned as Ali's face crumpled and a primal mewing sob escaped her mouth like an injured kitten. He pulled her against him, rocking and crooning, dropping kisses on her hair as she cried as if the end of the world were nigh.

Love, pure and simple, rose up in his chest and rippled through every cell in his body and he held her tighter as the thought terrified and tantalised in equal measure.

He wasn't ready for something like this. God alone knew he didn't need it. His heart was still battered from his divorce and he wanted to protect it from the slings and arrows of another love.

But somehow, she made it feel whole again.

The fact was undisputable—he loved Dr Aleisha Gregory. *With everything he had.*

'She okay?' Kat asked, interrupting Max's staggering revelation.

Max startled. *He wasn't sure about Ali but he knew he was far from okay!*

Ali pulled away from his chest with great reluctance. 'Sorry,' she murmured, avoiding his gaze as she patted at her damp cheeks. 'I'm fine.'

'Why don't you both come inside?' Kat suggested. 'You look like you need a good stiff drink.'

Ali would have liked nothing more. But even after a few minutes back in Max's arms her heart was already bleeding—she didn't want to sit opposite him and make small talk when all she'd want to do was drag him into the River Breeze storeroom and have her way with him.

She just had to get away from him.

'No.' She shook her head. 'I'm going to go home to bed if the boss will allow it. I forgot how exhausting an emergency can be.'

And going home was much safer than drinking under the influence of her sex-starved libido.

Max watched the bounce of her butterscotch curls and wished he could go home with her, but the mention of the emergency brought his reason for being here back into sharp focus. In all the excitement of the last half an hour, and particularly the last few minutes, he'd forgotten it entirely.

And he doubted very much she was going to welcome him into her bed after that particular piece of news.

But it still had to be done.

'Could I bum a lift back to my apartment?'

Ali shot him an alarmed look. *For crying out loud, why didn't he just leave her to suffer this one-sided love alone?*

'Don't you need the exercise?' she enquired stiffly.

The question seemed to require that she check him out for proof, which she did. But all she found was a vest top that sat snug against a broad chest and a flat male belly and solid masculine quads outlined to perfection in thigh-hugging skins.

None of them appeared to require exercise.

She dragged her gaze back to his face to find one eyebrow quirked at her.

Max smiled, encouraged by her interest. 'No.'

Ali fought a surge of desire at his staggering self-assurance and a wicked whisper urging her to push him into the dark clump of trees she could see in the background and kiss that smug smile right off his face.

Why? Why did she fall for emotionally unavailable men?

'Fine,' she huffed.

It was impossible to deny the man who had fought for her innocence such a simple request. But she didn't have to like it.

'Shall we go?' he asked as she continued to glare at him.

His lazy smile and deep voice swept over her like the long low note of a saxophone and went straight to her pelvic floor. 'Fine,' she muttered again.

* * *

Max waited until they'd been driving for a few minutes before he brought up the incident at the River Breeze again. He'd run through the whole situation in detail and was still blown away by her skill.

It was that or think about the other thing that had blown him away tonight and he couldn't do that with her sitting beside him as if she were made from concrete.

'It felt good, didn't it?' he said into the silence. 'Josh?'

Ali flinched internally at his insight and contemplated lying. The last thing she wanted to do was talk about her future with the one man who wasn't going to be part of it—it just hurt too damn much. But the glow from helping out with Josh still warmed her.

She nodded. 'I felt...normal again.' She lifted a hand off the steering wheel and pressed it to her chest as her heart beat a little faster at the memory of it all. 'Like a doctor again. I was nervous but...I knew...I just knew it was me.'

Max smiled at her profile. 'You never stopped being a doctor, Ali.'

She shook her head. 'I did in my heart.'

'No, you didn't. Your head maybe, but not your heart. Every day you were dishing out some piece of medical advice or other. A Band-Aid here, a mole check there. You've lived and breathed it, Ali. It's what you are. And you're too good at it to throw it all in and become a waitress or whatever the hell else takes your fancy for twenty-four hours.'

Ali felt tears at the backs of her eyes. She knew he was right. 'I know,' she whispered.

Max lifted a hand to her shoulder. 'Thank goodness,' he murmured.

She gave him a watery smile as she pulled up in front of his apartment complex and turned the ignition off. The glow from her foray back into medicine had dissipated with the knowledge that she had to go back and face her demons but another glow had taken over.

A very unwelcome one at that.

His hand on her shoulder was warm and heavy and causing havoc everywhere. His heady male scent filled her little car and she had to grip the steering wheel hard to stop her doing something crazy like leaning over and gnawing on his bare bicep.

It would be easy if it were just sexual attraction. But she needed more. She needed him to love her with the same soul-deep, wrenching agony she loved him. She needed his all.

Max, who had fought the urge to touch her, to drop his hand on her knee, run it up the length of her thigh, for the entire ten-minute car journey broke the growing silence. 'I've missed you, Ali.'

Ali shut her eyes. 'Don't.'

'Come up with me,' he murmured.

Ali shook her head against the illicit image of them making love one more time. 'No.'

'I know you said in your note that you think we were just distractions for each other but the truth is…I really like you, Ali.'

It was a complete understatement and an outright lie but he sensed she was poised to flee and he didn't want to frighten her away with the other L word.

Why would she believe him? She'd been hurt and scarred and was trying to get her life back on track. It was too much to dump on her tonight, especially following the huge revelation that medicine was her calling.

He needed to go slow with her. Woo her. Give her the time and space and support she needed. And hope that out of the attraction she felt for him, something stronger would grow.

Ali gripped the steering wheel tighter. She wanted to feel his mouth against hers again. Feel his weight on her, his hardness buried inside her. But she had her pride. She wouldn't accept crumbs from him.

Not when some other woman was getting the cake.

Max lifted his hand slowly and pushed a floppy curl out of her eye. He wanted to be able to erase the frown from her forehead. Love her with his body if that was all she allowed.

'Ali,' he whispered. He cupped her cheek and stroked the pad of his thumb along her cheekbone. 'Please, Ali.'

Sensing that she wanted it as much as he did, he moved in towards her, no longer able to resist the heady female smell of her that teased his nostrils and stoked his libido. He nuzzled her neck, inhaling deeply, dizzy with her scent. He licked up her neck, stroked his tongue over the lobe of her ear.

'I want to kiss you, Ali,' he murmured. 'I want to kiss you all night. Everywhere.'

Ali, hands still gripping the steering wheel, shut her eyes and her mind to his serpent-like treachery. She couldn't succumb. If she did, it was a slippery slope to oblivion.

'Let me love you, Ali.'

CHAPTER TWELVE

ALI whimpered at his choice of words. Not fair, not fair, she wanted to cry as all her resistance melted to liquid.

Yes, she knew he didn't mean *love*. But he was just too near, too irresistible, too damn Max.

Max heard the noise at the back of her throat and felt Ali tense. He cursed the slip of his tongue but it had seemed the most natural thing in the world to say.

For a second, he thought he'd lost her.

But then her hands dropped from the wheel and she turned her head and her lips were seeking his and then they were on him and she was opening to him, leaning closer, clutching at his shirt, moaning as his tongue duelled with hers.

The kiss ignited and in seconds they were pawing at each other like horny teenagers. The temperature rose a degree or two as their noisy ragged breathing fogged up the windows.

Max pulled away as Ali's fingers stroked

him through his shorts. He grabbed her hand, stopping the torture, but pressing it close, his head spinning from the delicious friction. 'My apartment,' he gasped. 'Now.'

Ali, her brain jumbled, her resistance melted, didn't even think of denying him. Of denying herself. She'd missed him. Missed this. She groped blindly for the door handle and stumbled out of the car.

Max was beside her, reaching for her hand, then hurrying her into the building. The lift was waiting for them and he dragged her in, not even waiting for the doors to close before he started kissing her again.

Ali hung on as he hiked her up the wall, balancing her on the cold metal hand rail. She locked her legs around his waist as the lift zoomed to the top floor and his kisses completely shorted out any rational thoughts. He kissed down her neck as his hands pushed under her T-shirt and boldly sought her breasts.

The lift arrived just as he freed one to his gaze and sucked hard on the puckered nipple. Ali threw back her head and cried out.

Then he was yanking her shirt down and lifting her off the hand rail and pulling her along behind him until they were at his door and then inside his door and then inside his bedroom.

'Take your clothes off,' he demanded, kissing her hard and deep as he pulled at his own.

His husky command and soul-drugging kiss made her legs go weak and she fumbled ineffectually with them. All that mattered was his mouth and the delicious havoc it was creating. Everything else was paralysed.

When Max finished with his clothes he worked on hers until she was finally naked, finally exposed to his greedy eyes, his greedy hands, his greedy mouth.

He pushed her back on his bed and watched as everything bounced and shifted just the way he liked it. 'God, I've missed you,' he whispered.

And then Ali reached for him and there were no more words, no more thoughts. Just moans and licks and gasps and whimpers. Delicious sensations sprinkling down on them like fairy dust. Holding on tight as their bodies moved to a rhythm uniquely theirs.

Building and building and building until they could no longer stay earthbound but flew up into the cosmos and floated amongst the stars.

Ali held onto Max, onto the stars, as long as she could. Even when he went to move off her she tightened her arms around him. 'No,' she protested. 'Not yet.'

She didn't want to ever let go. She wanted to imprint this moment on her brain for ever. Remember his weight and the warmth of his breath on her neck and the delicious sensation of him still being inside her.

Max held on tight trying to absorb her into his cells. He wanted to remember this moment too. Remember how his love was so over-whelming it felt as if it were spilling out of his pores, being released on his breath.

He bit down hard on the desire to tell her. It was too soon. She wasn't ready to hear it.

She shifted under him and he eased off, this time ignoring her protests. 'Shh,' he murmured, scooping her close, his hand automati-cally spearing into her hair, then running down the length of her spine and back up to her hair again.

Ali sighed as her orgasm and Max's magic touch lulled her doubts into oblivion. Her eye-lids fluttered closed. And it was in this drowsy state her subconscious threw up a nagging question.

She opened her eyes. 'Why were you there, tonight?' she murmured. 'At the River Breeze? You said you wanted to talk to me?'

Max's hand stilled on her shoulder blade for a moment before continuing its lazy path.

'Yes,' he murmured.

Ali felt him tense a little and held her breath

as her own lethargy dissipated in response. What had he wanted to talk to her about? Something personal maybe? Her silly heart tapped crazily in her chest.

She released her breath on a husky note. 'Oh?' she said, keeping her voice light. She shivered as his fingers stroked like feathers over her skin.

Max waited a few moments before he spoke. 'I got notice today from Palmerston and McGarrick.'

Ali frowned. Why was that name familiar? 'Who?'

Max kept stroking, wishing it were going to be enough to stop Ali from flipping out. 'The Cullens' lawyers. They've lodged an appeal.'

It took a moment for the words to register in Ali's brain, sluggish from Max's petting. Then they roared in her head like a trombone. She half sat up, using his chest as leverage. Her heart boomed in her ears. 'Seriously?'

Max nodded. 'An appeal was always on the cards if we won,' he said as he brushed her curls back off her shoulder.

Ali flinched at his touch as she stared down at him. *How could he be so calm?*

Because he was a man and the last time she'd depended on a man for emotional support when she'd needed it most, he'd walked out of her life and hadn't looked back. How could she have been so foolish to have expected Max to be any different?

She should have learned a year ago that she could only depend on herself. That she had to deal with these things on her own.

The thought was so depressing an uncharacteristic rage welled in her chest. *This wasn't fair—it just wasn't fair.* She'd been put through the wringer and every time she was vindicated another hearing, another court case reared its ugly head.

She swung her legs over the side of the bed and buried her face in her hands. 'This is never going to end, is it?' she despaired.

Max rolled up on his elbow, the defeated line of her back, the slump to her shoulders punching him hard in the gut. 'It won't be granted, Ali. It's going to be thrown out of court before it even gets that far.'

She turned her head to face him. 'How do you know?' she demanded.

He stroked a hand down her back. 'They have no grounds.'

Ali shrugged him away. 'That doesn't seem to have stopped them so far,' she shot back.

She looked back at the floor. Her undies and shirt were nearby and she reached for them. She stood, keeping her back to him, and stepped into her pants, then pulled her T-shirt down over her head.

Max watched her with dismay, ignoring the dictates of his body, which were urging him to drag her back down to the bed and pull her close. She'd just had her world yanked out from under her again. It was etched all over her face. Sex wasn't the answer.

'The appeal process is different, Ali. They don't have the grounds.'

Ali shook her head as she turned to face him. 'How do you know?' she demanded.

'It's my job, Ali. Just like you knew exactly what that boy needed tonight, how to help him, I know stuff to do with the law. You're a brilliant doctor. I'm a brilliant lawyer. Trust me.'

Except she was never going to get the chance to be a brilliant doctor, was she? Tears welled in her eyes and she dashed them away. This was all Max's fault. For telling her she was awesome, for insisting she shouldn't give up on medicine, for encouraging her to follow her calling, for shooting down every career choice she'd floated.

She'd bought into his fantasy only to have it crumble before she even got a chance to live it.

She'd worked on Josh tonight and had finally felt alive again. Finally known that medicine was in her marrow. Only to have it snatched away once more.

Max couldn't bear the sadness on her face. 'It won't get up,' he murmured.

She searched his face. 'What if it does?'

'It won't.'

Ali shook her head. She couldn't stay here, she had to get out. All she wanted was to have him hold her and tell her that he loved her. She couldn't bear that he didn't. Not now, not in her hour of need.

It was just like Tom all over again. She'd deal with the sickening prospect of the appeal by herself. At least she wouldn't feel let down. Betrayed.

And if she stayed, she might not be responsible for what she blurted out. She might even beg him to love her.

'I have to go.'

Max frowned. 'What?' He reached out a hand to her. 'Don't go. Not like this.'

Ali shrank from it. She couldn't bear for him to touch her, not without love. 'I'm fine,' she said tersely as the walls of her world crashed around her.

'Ali...don't. Let me help you.'

And that was when Ali lost it. He couldn't help her. In fact he'd just made things worse. So very much worse. He'd made her fall in love with him and made her want to be a doctor again.

She placed her hands on her hips and glared down at him. 'Help me? Help me?' she snorted.

'All you've done is made things worse,' she yelled.

She marched around his bed then, kicking aside discarded clothes looking for her bra and trousers.

Max sat up watching her stalk around the room, her curls bouncing, magnificent in her rage. She couldn't leave. Not like this. Not so angry.

Not at all if he had his way.

'It's going to be okay, Ali,' he said gently as she bent over to retrieve her trousers. She was angry and irrational—if he could just make her see it was going to be okay…

Ali's blood pressure hit the roof as she righted herself. She saw red with his Pollyanna views and his 'don't frighten the horses' voice.

'It's not going to be okay,' she snapped. 'It's never going to be okay again.'

Everything from the last year, all the upheaval and disappointments and losses—her baby, her poor darling baby—welled up in her at once. A lump of what felt like molten rock seemed lodged in under her ribcage and was growing larger with each breath.

'There are two things at the very beginning I told you I wasn't going to do,' she yelled, shaking her trousers at him. 'Get back into medicine and fall for another man. And you've made me break both those.'

Ali watched as Max's grey eyes widened. *Crap!* Now she'd completely humiliated herself. She rubbed at her chest. It was tight, impossibly tight; she could barely breathe.

Max stilled. 'What did you say?'

A tear escaped and she couldn't even be bothered to dash it away. She might as well make the humiliation complete.

'And then,' she yelled, ignoring him, 'when you get me excited about medicine again and you make me fall in love with you, you snatch them both back!'

Max frowned. *She loved him?* Did she just say she loved him? 'What?' He shook his head. 'How?'

'By telling me about the appeal,' she cried. 'And by still being in love with your wife.'

Max blinked. *What the—?* He raised himself to his haunches and held out his hand in a stopping motion. 'What on earth are you talking about?'

Ali could feel the hot tears flowing out of her eyes thick and fast now as she attempted to step into her trousers. 'I saw you,' she accused as she missed the leg hole and made a second attempt. 'With Pete on the deck that morning. Remember? I could hear everything from the sink. About Tori. The baby.'

Her own womb contracted at the thought.

She wanted a baby, damn it. She wanted it with a ferocity that almost winded her.

She wanted Max's baby.

She sucked in a shaky breath. 'I saw how devastated you were.' Both legs were in now and she yanked the trousers up to her waist. 'I heard it in your voice. Only a man who's still in love with a woman would be so gutted.'

Max shook his head. 'You're wrong.'

'Am I?' she demanded, dashing away the tears. 'Are you sure it wasn't really her you were making love to after Pete left while you were having sex with me?'

Ali glared at him. She wanted to hurt him as much as she was hurting. She yanked her zipper up with a vicious tug.

The noise was as loud as a slap in the silence and Max reared back as if it had been. Her ugly suggestion made him want to cross the floor and shake her.

'I am not still in love with my *ex*-wife.'

Max's voice dropped to a low growl and Ali felt the hairs on the back of her neck rise. But she was damned if she was going to back down. Everything was a mess and it felt good to have someone else to blame for a change instead of herself.

'Well, you could have fooled me,' she snapped.

Max threw back the sheet and stepped out of bed. He picked up his underwear off the floor and put it on. His heart was pounding. *She loved him.* She'd said she loved him. It was his turn to be honest.

To hell with waiting. To hell with her not being ready.

He shoved his hands on his hips and glared at her. 'I'm in love with you.'

It was Ali's turn to rear back. She gasped. Her silly, silly heart leapt at his words. But her brain was in control. Her heart had got her into too much trouble in the past.

'No.' She shook her head wildly. She wouldn't open up her heart again. She wouldn't be fooled. 'I saw it—I saw your face. You're still in love with Tori.'

Max stood his ground. 'I was in shock, Ali. That's all. I was stunned…bewildered. But not because I still love her or have any lingering feelings for her—believe me, I fell out of love with Tori a long time ago. Because it was unexpected. Totally out of left-field. Because she'd so vehemently not wanted a baby. Finding out she was pregnant was a shock. And, yes, it hurt. But not my heart, Ali. It hurt my ego, my pride.'

Ali's heart lifted again. She so wanted to believe him. But she quashed it ruthlessly. 'So you're telling me if she waltzed back through that door, right now, wanting to try again, you wouldn't take her back?'

Max put his hand on his heart. 'That's right.'

'Even if she wanted to have babies with you?'

Max kept his hand firmly in place. 'That's right.'

'Even if she got on her knees and begged.'

Max nodded his head. 'I wish her well. I hope she's very happy. But the only woman I'm interested in having babies with is you.'

Ali's breath caught in her throat. The sincerity blazing in his steady grey eyes was humbling. 'You want babies with me?'

Ali heard her voice crack a little as another hot tear welled up and spilled down her cheek. The deep empty place inside her filled up with a wonderful warm glow.

Max dropped his hand and took a step towards her. 'In time, sure. Lots of babies. Lots and lots.'

She halted him with a wave of her hand. A part of her wanted to leap in his arms, to rejoice in this startling turn of events. To believe him. But the saner part, the part that had taken too many knocks this past year, that had been unbearably hurt, couldn't believe that something was going right for once.

The thought of opening up her heart again was utterly terrifying. 'I don't understand,' she said suspiciously. 'When did this big revelation occur?'

Max looked at his watch. 'About six hours ago.'

Tonight? He'd only just realised tonight. Ali took a step back. 'That was rather convenient,' she said, her voice full of starch.

Max pushed a hand through his hair. She was scared, he understood that. Frankly he was pretty damn terrified himself. He knew how much it took when you'd already been hurt to put yourself out there and love someone else again. But love didn't let you choose.

He had to convince her. Because as terrifying as it was to love her, it was more terrifying not to.

'I was watching you with that boy and you were so incredible, so…amazing and then you burst into tears and I was holding you and I knew, I just suddenly knew that you were the most precious thing in the whole world to me. It was truly one of those biblical kind of things.'

Ali smiled for the first time since she'd leapt out of bed. Here they were in a state of undress yelling at each other after having just had hot sweaty sex and he was going all biblical.

'Biblical huh?'

Max smiled too. 'I saw the light.' He took a step towards her. 'Although in retrospect I think it was probably that first night. When you said fish were cute. I think I started falling right then and there.'

Ali grinned. It seemed like a hundred years ago now.

Max moved closer again. When she didn't object he took another step. 'How about you?' he asked.

Ali's smile faded as she remembered her own particularly horrible revelation that awful day Pete had come to visit. 'In your apartment that morning. When Pete was talking to you about Tori and you looked so gutted. That's when I realised.'

'Ouch.' Max took another step closer. *Nearly there.* 'So that's why you left.'

Ali nodded. 'I couldn't bear being with you knowing that you loved someone else. I'd already been down that road, Max. I couldn't do it again.'

Max nodded as he slid his hand around her waist tentatively. When she didn't protest he tugged her gently to him.

'You won't have to, Ali. I'm your guy. Your one-woman guy.'

Ali placed her hands on his biceps, her body already melting against the heat of him. She looked into his grey eyes, still trying to keep a hold of the door to her heart. 'Isn't that what we all think when we first get together, Max? Isn't that what you thought with Tori? It's what I thought with Tom. How do we know that we're not doomed to failure?'

Max smiled as he fingered that persistent floppy curl out of her eye. 'I guess we don't, ultimately. That's what makes love such a leap of faith. But I've never felt this deeply about anyone, not even Tori. And I know I want to be with your for ever. So what do you say? I'm ready to jump. Jump with me?'

Ali felt her throat clog with emotion. He was right. Love was a leap of faith. The door crashed open and she let the love flow out.

'Oh, Max. I love you so much. I'll jump with you anywhere.'

Max stared into the eyes of the woman he loved and felt whole for the first time in a long time. He dropped a kiss on her forehead, her nose, her cheek and a long lingering one on her mouth.

When he drew back they were both breathing hard. 'Come back to bed,' he whispered. 'Let's make love.'

Ali smiled at him. 'Mmm, I like the sound of that.'

'Good,' he said, nuzzling her neck. 'Because I'm going to spend a lifetime making love to you.'

Ali laughed. 'In that case, I'm going to spend a lifetime letting you.'

* * * * *

Read on for a sneak preview of Carol Marinelli's
PUTTING ALICE BACK TOGETHER!

Hugh hired bikes!

You know that saying: 'It's like riding a bike, you never forget'?

I'd never learnt in the first place.

I never got past training wheels.

'You've got limited upper-body strength?' He stopped and looked at me.

I had been explaining to him as I wobbled along and tried to stay up that I really had no centre of balance. I mean *really* had no centre of balance. And when we decided, fairly quickly, that a bike ride along the Yarra perhaps, after all, wasn't the best activity (he'd kept insisting I'd be fine once I was on, that you never forget), I threw in too my other disability. I told him about my limited upper-body strength, just in case he took me to an indoor rock-climbing centre next. I'd honestly forgotten he was a doctor, and he seemed worried, like I'd had a mini-stroke in the past or had mild cerebral palsy or something.

'God, Alice, I'm sorry—you should have said. What happened?'

And then I had had to tell him that it was a self-diagnosis. 'Well, I could never get up the ropes at the gym at school.' We were pushing our bikes back. 'I can't blow-dry the back of my hair...' He started laughing.

Not like Lisa who was laughing at me—he was just laughing and so was I. We got a full refund because we'd only been on our bikes ten minutes, but I hadn't failed. If anything, we were getting on better.

And better.

We went to St Kilda to the lovely bitty shops and I found these miniature Russian dolls. They were tiny, made of tin or something, the biggest no bigger than my thumbnail. Every time we opened them, there was another tiny one, and then another, all reds and yellows and greens.

They were divine.

We were facing each other, looking down at the palm of my hand, and our heads touched.

If I put my hand up now, I can feel where our heads touched.

I remember that moment.

I remember it a lot.

Our heads connected for a second and it was alchemic; it was as if our minds kissed hello.

I just have to touch my head, just there at the very spot and I can, whenever I want to, relive that moment.

So many times I do.

'Get them.' Hugh said, and I would have, except that little bit of tin cost more than a hundred dollars and, though that usually wouldn't have stopped me, I wasn't about to have my card declined in front of him.

I put them back.

'Nope.' I gave him a smile. 'Gotta stop the impulse

spending.'

We had lunch.

Out on the pavement and I can't remember what we ate, I just remember being happy. Actually, I can remember: I had Caesar salad because it was the lowest carb thing I could find. We drank water and I *do* remember not giving it a thought.

I was just thirsty.

And happy.

He went to the loo and I chatted to a girl at the next table, just chatted away. Hugh was gone for ages and I was glad I hadn't demanded Dan from the universe, because I would have been worried about how long he was taking.

Do I go on about the universe too much? I don't know, but what I do know is that something *was* looking out for me, helping me to be my best, not to **** this up as I usually do. You see, we walked on the beach, we went for another coffee and by that time it was evening and we went home and he gave me a present.

Those Russian dolls.

I held them in my palm, and it was the nicest thing he could have done for me.

They are absolutely my favourite thing and I've just stopped to look at them now. I've just stopped to take them apart and then put them all back together again and I can still feel the wonder I felt on that day.

He was the only man who had bought something for me, I mean something truly special. Something beautiful, something thoughtful, something just for me.

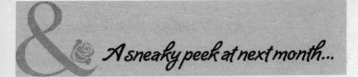

A sneaky peek at next month...

RIVA™

LIVE LIFE TO THE FULL – GIVE IN TO TEMPTATION

My wish list for next month's titles...

In stores from 2nd March 2012:

☐ The Good, the Bad and the Wild – Heidi Rice

☐ Mr Right at the Wrong Time – Nikki Logan

☐ When Chocolate Is Not Enough... – Nina Harrington

Available at WHSmith, Tesco, Asda, Eason, Amazon and Apple

Just can't wait?

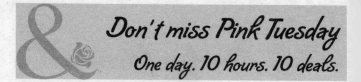
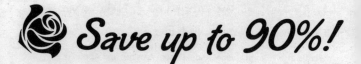